PRAISE FOR **OLYMPIA KNIFE**

"[STARRED REVIEW]… Americans don't have fairy tales: we have legends. Tall tales. [The world of *Olympia Knife*] is vibrant, dangerous, and a smart commentary on social prejudices against outsiders. Queer, differently-abled, fat, and nonwhite characters pack the pages. Set in the postbellum South, *Olympia Knife* is, at its core, a story about a culture that is no longer able to ignore its own diversity or the itch for change. Author Alysia Constantine is a superb writer whose distinctive, rich style makes *Olympia Knife* a pleasure from beginning to end."

—*Foreword Reviews*

"FOUR STARS… The world of *Olympia Knife* is one that goes beyond genre definitions and expectations. It's a deft historical fantasy romance that addresses issues of queerness and marginalization through the lens of a tight-knit traveling circus. Constantine's writing is evocative; it reads like a tale being told over a crackling campfire… [*Olympia Knife* is] a gentle historical fantasy with a hint of magic, perfect for readers who love queer romances and books such as *Tipping the Velvet* or *Water For Elephants*."

—*RT Book Reviews*

PRAISE FOR **SWEET**

"[STARRED REVIEW]… all romance, endlessly surprising, and nothing like any genre offering this season."

—*Publishers Weekly*

2016 Foreword Indies Award Honorable Mention for LGBT Literature

"FOUR STARS… The narrative quality is unique. Readers who are looking for a new way to tell a romance story will really enjoy how the narrator breaks the fourth wall and speaks directly to them… If you are looking for a sugary read with a dash of pain and healing, pick this one up. Once you get into it, you'll find yourself unable to stop."

—*RT Book Reviews*

"4.75 STARS… Every once in a while a book comes along that is not what was expected. *Sweet* falls into that category for me and I was thoroughly entertained, moved, and riveted during the time I spent with this book."

—*Joyfully Jay Reviews*

ALYSIA CONSTANTINE

Olympia Knife

interlude ❖ press • new york

This book is for all of us queer folk—not just those of us who are LGBTQ, but all of us who, because of the shape or ability of our bodies, because of our needs or our choices, live unseen, untethered, or outside the margins. Keep on keeping on, friends, because the world desperately needs us to stick around, even if most of its people don't seem to know it. It is, in most of the world—certainly in my corner of it—a particularly hard time for folks on the margins. But keep on. Even when smaller minds prevail, keep on. When meaning is twisted, when speech is unmoored from truth, when you know that no one will see you, when gravity fails, keep on. Even when the world is upended, when hate scrapes you up and things look most dire, even then, friends, even then, please, keep on.

Most especially, this book is for B——, with all my love and thanks for your kindness and strength. Somehow, you maintain an unwavering belief in me. I may be the Greek, but you're the Olympia.

"All that is solid melts into air, all that is holy is profaned, and man is at last compelled to face with sober senses… his relations with his kind."

—Karl Marx and Friedrich Engels

Some readers may find some of the scenes in this book difficult to read. We have compiled a list of content warnings, which you can access at www.interludepress.com/trigger-warnings

One
The Flying Knifes

THE NIGHT HER PARENTS DISAPPEARED for good, Olympia Knife was watching.

She sat on the high platform with her legs dangling into the dark below and waited for her father to swing up, grab her ankles, and hurl her through the dark air to her mother's arms. The noise of the crowd and the hooting calliope filtered up and mixed with the faint-but-never-gone tent smell of elephants and sweat and mildew.

Alban and Julia, The Flying Knifes, glinted silver like fish in the filmy dark, gaining speed and height with each dip of the trapeze. They called to each other, low enough that the crowd below couldn't hear: *Next one, love! Hup! Fly!*

Sequined backs arching across the distance, Alban and Julia swung forward and stretched their arms toward one another. This moment was an ache, a longing, an imminence Olympia loved, the seconds suspended and stretching toward the inevitable moment when their hands would meet. The calliope held its breath. The crowd clenched. The moment Alban and Julia touched, there was a blaring flash of light like a cymbal crash, a dazzle of sequins, and they were, suddenly, gone.

The whole night froze in waiting. The upturned faces were still and luminous as pebbles under water. The swings dangled empty, only faintly creaking. Even the crickets outside went still until, in the next moment, everything broke into calamity. All at once, the crowd began to holler, and spotlights flew in crazy, searching circles. Riggers and clowns and tumblers clambered up the ladder until the platform shook with their urgent flinging and slamming. Someone grabbed Olympia's waist and pulled her to his chest until everything was rough cotton and alcohol smell, and they were dropping down, like a heart falling, to the net below.

THE AUDIENCE HAD EMPTIED OUT of the tent. The benches bare, the lights too bright, the grass trampled, the tent was vast and desolate. Crickets, in the quiet, returned to their chirring. That night Olympia slept in fits, curled in an open bin of costumes to be mended, while everyone else searched to find a body, a shoe, a sequin, a drop of sweat, some evidence of the vanishing Knifes.

They found nothing.

* * *

ALBAN AND JULIA FELL IN love before they spoke the same language.

Alban spoke only English, with a heavy Scottish accent—nearly impossible for non-Scots to decipher under the best of circumstances. When he got excited, his neck would flush red and his speech would race past the vowels so fast he sounded as if he were choking, and not a soul in the circus knew what he meant unless he employed a series of wild gesticulations (which he always did).

In the sticky-hot summer of 1888, Julia had come from France with a group of other wealthy young women whose parents had sent them on a tour of the States to find husbands. On their outing to see the circus, she had become enamored of the dashing, redheaded tumbler immediately. When Julia lingered outside his trailer in the hour after the show, Alban brashly—because he was usually brash—burst into the courtyard, pumped her arm vigorously, nodded at her red-faced compliments in halting English, and promptly invited her to dinner.

Though she spoke only French, Julia understood, from the way he smiled and wound his arm around her waist and guided her toward the gathering tent, that he intended to take her to dinner with the rest of the crew. She went.

Through dinner, she smiled shyly while Alban waved his arms in the air as if to stir up the rapid babble of words he spilled endlessly (full mouth be damned) over the general hubbub of the community meal. Minnie, who, onstage, was known as the Fat Lady, smiled at them slyly, because anyone could see Alban was falling in love, and it looked to everyone as if Julia were happily falling as well. Shy as she was, she was drawn out by Alban until she giggled and sparkled, though most likely she understood none of the conversation. When Robin the Rubber Boy leapt to the tabletop at the end of the meal and entertained the crowd with his over-dramatic impressions of stage actors (who were, as a matter of course, made very flexible, always bending strangely or reaching for something), Julia laughed and clapped along with everyone else. When Robin, in his passion, kicked a glass of water into her lap, Julia jumped up, righted the glass, and mopped the table with her petticoat, then brushed the water from her dress and sat back down.

"Ai, lussey, yeh garta wibetta warteronyeh," Alban told her.

Julia shook her head and widened her eyes, until Minnie took pity on her and translated by pointing to the empty water glass, then to Julia's dress, saying, "A wee bit, a wee bit, *un peu*," as emphatically as she could.

Madame Barbue, the Bearded Lady, who could have easily translated since she had descended from a family of French-Canadian fur trappers, sat back and chuckled happily at the scene. Julia smiled and stood again to brush her skirt, but Alban was on his knees in front of her with a cloth and a very red face, dabbing at the dress and looking entirely scandalized, before she could think what to do.

By the end of the evening, through Alban's ceaselessly cheerful teaching, Julia had learned a few cautious words of English, and her heart had bloomed for the first time in her young life. At the end of the evening, he kissed her gently on the back of her hand, and she understood from this that she was to come find him before she traveled back to France.

Somehow, though they shared no language between them, Julia and Alban had fallen recklessly, intensely in love.

In a week, Julia went home to Hautefaye to say her goodbyes and carefully pack her dresses and shoes and books and her only piece of jewelry (a gorgeous filigreed hair comb), boarded another ship, and set sail back to America to join the circus and marry the tumbler Alban.

In just over a year, their daughter (a tiny, squalling, black-haired little thing Alban and Julia feared more than loved) was born. They called her Olympia, because the name portended greatness, and Julia had powerful secret hope for her, though Olympia was shriveled and weak and most often shook with helpless tears, even in Julia's own arms. And so Olympia Knife came into the world misnamed and misunderstood, but fiercely and completely loved by everyone she knew.

From the moment of her birth, Olympia was never permitted stillness. She was passed from arm to arm at the group meals, both so that Julia could have a moment to eat and so that everyone could have the chance to cuddle such a delicate, precious thing. Alban and Julia gently tossed her, still wink-eyed and swaddled in blankets, between them to ready her for the swings high in the tent top. To calm her for sleep, her mother rocked her vigorously in her arms, swinging the baby high above her head until Olympia fell asleep. She quickly grew accustomed to movement, and stillness frightened her. Julia was forced to rock and dance while she fed her or tried to hush her crying, because the moment she stopped moving, tiny Olympia would throw herself into furious fits of screaming.

It was terrifying when Olympia cried, far more so than when any other baby did, because when Olympia cried, she disappeared. The first time it happened, Julia was alone in the trailer with Olympia, trying to get her to nurse. It had been a difficult time; Olympia didn't seem to be able to figure out how to latch on to Julia's breast, no matter what Julia tried. Everyone had a suggestion, even those who had never been near a baby, but none of the suggestions worked. Minnie had rubbed Julia's breasts with butter in a last-ditch and rather creative effort to entice Olympia to latch, but nothing had come of it except a slippery mess (both Julia and Olympia had to be washed after that experiment) and a sick feeling in Julia's heart.

Julia was alone with the baby. She dropped into the rocking chair they'd placed next to the crib, held Olympia—who was screaming as if she were being ripped apart—against her chest, and wept. She was tired and numb from the baby's crying, and her breasts stung from all the abuse they'd suffered when she tried everyone's nursing suggestions. The baby was as good as dead if she wouldn't eat, Julia knew; she could feel the tiny body withering and growing thinner by the minute. Julia murmured to the baby, desperate pleas and enticements and encouragements in French, while trying to keep her own hysterical tears at bay. It was enough that Olympia was crying; if someone came into the trailer and found the two of them wailing together, they would surely take the baby away and lock Julia up in an asylum.

Suddenly, Julia's arms appeared to be entirely empty, though she could still hear the baby's crying and feel her weight on her chest. She felt Olympia's fists punch and twist the delicate skin of her neck, felt her shiver with sobs, and heard her plain as day, but when she looked, nothing was there. Olympia had disappeared.

Julia was so stunned that her tears dried instantly and her cries became shouts. She called for Alban or Minnie or anyone to come help. It was clear that Olympia was still *there* somehow—she could feel her struggling, thrashing weight, but couldn't see her. Balancing Olympia in one arm, she tried washing her own eyes with water until they stung, to no avail. She held the howling baby tighter, trying to soothe a melody out of her own voice, but it came out strangled with fear and only made the baby cry harder.

"Alban!" she yelled. "*Aidez-moi! Aidez-moi!* No eyes!"

In moments, the trailer door burst open, and Alban was there, red and breathing hard, with Minnie the Fat Lady behind him.

5

"Julia!" he breathed, rushing to her. "What's wrong? Where's the baby?"

Julia burst into tears again and indicated her eyes. "No eyes!" she howled. "*Aveugle!* No eyes!"

Alban looked confused, but Minnie rushed to her side and held her arm.

"Julia, calm down, *calme-toi*, love." She rubbed Julia's back. "Can you see me?"

Julia nodded tearfully. "Can you see Alban? Can you see the cot?"

"*Oui*," Julia said. "I see it."

"You're not blind, sweetheart. *N'es pas aveugle. Calme-toi.* Where is Olympia?"

Julia only wailed harder and held up her arms, which would have seemed to be empty were it not for the desperate screaming of the baby. Horrified, Minnie put her hand to her mouth. Alban began to search the crib, and the bed, and all the cupboards.

"Julia! Wartevya done?!" He overturned the crib, searched their own bed, rummaged through every cupboard. The baby continued to scream; Alban still could not find her. Julia stood, tears streaking her cheeks, and held her arms out, looking more and more desperate.

"*Non*, Alban!" She thrust her arms at him, but Alban would not stop.

"Get back!" Alban pushed her aside—the first time in their lives together that he'd been anything but absolutely loving and kind—and Julia began to sob harder. The baby continued to scream, and the racket only made Alban angrier and more desperate. Minnie pulled Julia into her arms to comfort her, but when she did, both Julia's and the baby's weeping grew louder.

"*Oui!*" Julia pressed her arms against Minnie. She looked wild. "Yes, yes, here!"

Minnie felt it, then: the scratch of tiny nails and the clutch of meaty little fists she couldn't see. She stopped, looked at Julia in awe, and then touched the baby in Julia's arms. She was there, she could feel her there; she knew it, but she couldn't see her.

"Yes!" Julia urged again. "Yes! Here!" She took Minnie's hand and placed it in the empty air by her shoulder, except that Minnie could feel—absolutely—the baby's face, hot and wet with saliva and tears. Minnie ran her hand around the face, then up to feel Olympia's soft hair, then down her back to feel the full weight of her scrawny body. She pinched what felt like a knee, and she heard the baby yelp.

Julia sniffled and held out her arms, and Minnie felt the baby's body, suddenly, in her own arms. Olympia's sobs quieted and she snuggled into the curve of Minnie's neck. Minnie put her hand on her back, commenced rubbing, and began to pace.

"Alban," she said quietly to the man, who was tearing up the trailer in his desperate search. "Alban!" Minnie said more firmly. She repeated his name until he stopped and looked at her.

"Alban, Olympia is here."

*   *   *

As she grew, Olympia was given sewing lessons by Minnie and Robin the Rubber Boy, who had earned his first name by learning to imitate, perfectly, every known bird of the regions in which they traveled. Dead-Eyed Susan taught her to poach chickens from farmyards using only a bow and arrow and a pleasant, innocent smile. Alban taught her to read in English and to scrawl careful, shaky letters with a stick in the dust; Julia taught her to speak French; Madame Barbue schooled her in proper comportment and good grooming.

When Olympia disappeared—and she did, on occasion, though she was visible most of the time—everyone had come to expect it and rarely worried or even noticed at all. When she was very afraid, or very angry, or even sometimes when she was very happy, it would happen (on her fifth birthday, laughing in delight at the antics of the clowns who put on a show just for her, she blinked out, and, for five minutes, everyone could hear Olympia laughing, but nobody could see her). She couldn't control it, and usually it took a moment or two to realize it had happened at all. Her first clue was often the surprise of the people around her. She herself felt nothing when she disappeared.

Once she had calmed down sufficiently, she would fade back into sight. She could do nothing to control it—nothing to make it happen or prevent it or even end it sooner. She learned, from Julia's and Alban's careful instruction, never to throw a tantrum in front of others, lest she suddenly disappear. When an audience watched the Knifes on their trapezes, she kept her cool and would not let herself be afraid; she learned not to laugh too excitedly, nor cry too terribly hard, and never to get angry in public—if she did so, she risked fading away and causing alarm. She learned as a matter of safety to keep herself carefully controlled at all times, and lived in the world as dampened and flat as she could make herself.

Alban and Julia had taught Olympia to fly, to leap from the safety of the high platform and hurl herself into open air because they would always, always catch her. But they also taught her that there were things from which they could not protect her and that she too must protect herself, and hide her difference as carefully as she was able. She lived in fear of losing control. She understood, as most children do not, that she was at the mercy of her body's whims, and could do nothing to change her situation except keep herself calm and, when she couldn't, learn to live with the fact that nobody—not a soul—could see her.

But among her circus family, this disappearing became, like Minnie's fatness or Arnold's shortness or Madame Barbue's beard, just another quality of a person whom everyone loved dearly. Held safely amongst them all, Olympia grew up capable and smart and very well-loved and, at least for the times she was visible, carefully watched over.

* * *

THREE DAYS AFTER HER PARENTS vanished in midair, three days spent in weeping stillness, flickering in and out of visibility, there remained nowhere Olympia could go that was not solemn and haunted and far too still. The empty swings, her parents' empty trailer, empty chairs and empty bed—not a space remained that was not chilled and stagnant. The tent where the Knifes had performed only reminded her of the rush of air on her cheeks and the drop of gravity in her stomach that she would, she was sure, never feel again. The circus folk fussed at her sleeve and followed her with kindly, mournful looks even to the woods, even to the door of her trailer, where they sat in vigil on the step when she shut them out.

The absence and the stillness were everywhere, and so, the very moment she turned sixteen, in the cricket-quiet night, Olympia packed a loaf of bread, a block of cheese, and a crock of water and hid them by the woods' edge. She waited for the circus to open the next day, and for everyone around her to grow too busy to notice, before she slipped into the raucous Saturday afternoon crowd. She picked pockets for coins nobody would miss and let the wave of people carry her out of the circus and toward the train yard, then hid by the tracks until a good train—slow-moving, whistling brightly, with open boxcars—wound down into the valley and then she tossed her bag onto an empty car and leapt after it.

She hid there for days, peeling at the wooden wall with her pocketknife as the train jiggled through the muggy almost-July heat. She knocked her boot in rhythm with the snap of the train on the tracks and recited the names of the towns through which the train passed, the names of everyone she knew, every poem Alban and Julia had ever forced her to memorize in her schooling. She rocked in nauseated, sweaty sleep. She smelled rotting apples and manure and dust. She watched fields of butterfly weed and spindly trees and little, lonely houses whisk up and away from view until the train finally slowed to a rumbling crawl in Louisiana and she jumped.

She found work as a seamstress and cook on a rambling property near Lake Pontchartrain, assisting William and Margaret Henry, a hearty and staunchly open-minded couple who ran a small press, composing and distributing leaflets (*The Working Class Shall Become the Ruling Class! Sisters, Raise Your Voices: Demand the Vote!*). She learned from William how to run and clean the press and spent several very long nights with the two of them, helping to crank the ink-belching print wheel and hang freshly printed leaflets to dry. The palms of her hands, within a couple weeks, were stained black with ink.

Every day was inevitable and still; the only uncertainty was in the news they printed on broadsheets several nights a month. Olympia slept, like William and Margaret, through most mornings and well into the heat of the afternoon, when she would rouse herself to do the little bit of cooking and cleaning they asked of her before the three of them shut themselves in the back office, where Margaret set the type and William cranked the press and Olympia cut and hung the wet prints.

When the Henrys held a salon for their friends—schooled and brilliant, wealthy, smug, but still kind—Margaret always made sure that Olympia was asked to join. She would sit and listen, over tea she'd brewed and biscuits she'd baked, while William and Margaret and their friends talked over causes about which Olympia cared little and politicians of whom she knew nothing. She felt like the lucky child who had been allowed to stay up and listen while her parents entertained, and drowsed happily in a corner armchair as the adults hub-bubbed their smartest conversation. She always concentrated upon keeping herself calm and only mildly happy so that she would not draw attention and cause panic by blinking out of sight—until, inevitably, William or Margaret would turn to her and proudly nod in her direction.

"Olympia has been to South Carolina, haven't you, Olympia? She's traveled most of the States," William or Margaret would say, gesturing her way with a flourish.

"Yes," she'd whisper, and sit straight as she could in her chair, clearing her throat to raise her voice and *not disappearing, not at all disappearing.* "Except the West. Every year in South Carolina, we set up in Saluba and Berkeley."

At the guests' puzzled looks, Margaret would whisper to the group, "She used to perform in a traveling circus!" The revelation was always followed by murmurs of surprise and interest from the others.

"What did you do, dear?" someone would always ask.

"The Flying Knifes," Olympia would say, and someone would say, "My! How daring!" and someone else would cry, "Sounds quite dangerous!" and Olympia would have to explain that there were no actual knives in the act, that "Knife" was the family name, and then feebly protest about safety and nets and training. But Olympia did so mostly to herself, because by then the conversation had babbled on well past the curiosities of circus life and back to questions of the rights of women and the poor.

She stayed with the Henrys until her arms and legs began to itch and she couldn't sleep at night. The fields, the house, the sky, the lake, everything was the same stagnant shade of brownish green. One afternoon, as she hung wet linens on a line outside the big house, the itch grew louder in her bones, almost a rattling soreness, and she had to *move*. She paced the line from end to end under the pretense of evening its weight, stopping every few paces to scratch and slap her humming skin, but the itch became a buzzing that traveled up from her ankles past her knees and into the meat of her thighs. The moment she stood still, her shoes began to sink and the dirt and stones began to pile in mounds around her legs. She kicked and jumped to new earth, but the second she stood still again, the earth crawled over her feet and up her legs anew. If she did not move again, she would be swallowed up in minutes. Olympia slapped at her legs until she could no longer stand it; then she turned and fled.

She left behind two dresses, cast off by the lady of the house and carefully mended into her own shape; the schoolbook and writing paper Margaret had given her when she caught Olympia stealing a pen and ink from the study; and the cache of mica-flecked rocks collected from the lake bottom on those mornings when she bathed in solitude there. She also left a note on the doorstep for the kind couple who had given her work and taught her to improve her reading and writing and allotted her a goose feather bed in the hayloft: *I've gone back. I will send a letter.* Then she walked, empty as a pocket, down the road, knowing she would never send the letter, no matter how good her intentions. She walked until she found the train south and bought a ticket, hoping to catch the circus on its annual autumn retreat into the warmth of Florida.

When she found the little troupe, she walked into the gathering tent and was immediately drawn into one warm embrace after another, then put to work washing the tin plates from the evening meal as if she were only returning from a day trip to town. Despite the riotous greeting she received, once the kisses and cries and embraces were finished, the tent felt desolate, the dinner quiet, the food sparse. Since her parents' disappearance, many of the crew had gone, too, and the circus had lost, for good, Kirby the Human Pincushion as well as Athena and Dimitri the animal trainers, who had left behind the white horses of Arabia, the two tigers, and a kangaroo straight from the Wilds of Africa, all of which had languished in their cages because even Ramus the Strongest Man Alive was too scared to go nearer than was necessary to toss the furious animals their food through the locked bars). The twelve-clown act, which made up the vast majority of the remaining circus folk, were a sour and separatist—and largely unhelpful—lot, and may as well not have been there at all.

Since the Flying Knifes were long gone and had been replaced by a troupe of acrobats who worked on the trapeze, it was quickly and unanimously decided that Olympia would walk the high-wire. Up on the wire near the top of the tent, the work would be lonely but, at least, familiar.

* * *

New broadsides, billing her as "Olympia Knife, The Girl Who Walks on Air," were printed. The barker, a crewman called Bale who stood outside the big tent to cajole and tease the crowds in, began to hone his new call: "Ladies, she will still your Hearts with her Risk-Walking! Gentlemen, she will still your Hearts, too [*and here he winked broadly*], but not with her Daring alone! Come see our shapely and wholesome Fearless Beauty, Olympia, Goddess of the High Wire!"

Minnie, who was known onstage as the Fat Lady but who, when the rubes were gone, was simply known as Minnie—and the troupe's best seamstress—sewed Olympia a new dress and a pair of ruffled bloomers which peeked out of the very short skirt at the knee. The bodice was dusted with sequins and ruffled with heavy lace and billowing sleeves, and the shoes were suede-soled, cobbled of peach-soft leather and satin (made lovingly by hand for her by The World's Smallest Major General Tiny Napoleon Only Three Feet Tall, who, onstage, affected an officious air and a French accent, but whom, backstage, everyone simply called Arnold). The shoes were tied with ribbons and glass beads so that Olympia could easily walk the wire, yes, but also so that her ankles sparkled and all attention would be on her feet as she walked. On her head was fastened a headband with a large satin bow, intricately accented with lace and sequins and sparkling fringe. Similarly spangled ribbons were tied around each of her wrists and the whole kit was topped off with a ridiculously large white ostrich feather secured to her headband, where it bobbed softly in the air two feet above her head. Olympia felt, once she'd been stuffed and tied into the frothy pink-and-cream concoction, quite like an exploded, glittering, and over-sweet birthday cake.

Still, in the heat of the Florida afternoon, she practiced on a low cable strung between two poles outside the tent, as Minnie and a crowd of other performers watched, occasionally suggesting small improvements to heighten the drama (a flourish here, a fumble and almost-slip there). She worked doggedly until she was exhausted and panting and the soles of her feet stung from gripping the cable, but, even though she would perform with a net, she was terrified of erring and falling and the terror made her fade to a dimly flickering girl every time her foot touched the wire. Her stomach turned: She would take the act to the high-wire in less than a week.

* * *

ON THE NIGHT OF HER first show, some of the performers left a basket of bread on her doorstep—this was tradition—and she ate a small piece for luck—also tradition—before slipping into the back entrance of the tent to wait and watch the show.

On the swings were The World-Famous Russian Aerialists, The Mirnov Family, who were almost none of those things: not famous, nor family, nor—most of them—Russian. Olympia watched them fling from swing to swing in their sparkling white suits (made to catch the light just so) and heard their movements punctuated by the smack-and-grip of their hands when they grabbed the swing bars or each other's arms. She knew, but could not hear, that they were grunting and sweating as they worked, that they called soft instructions to one another in crisp English, and that the swings were becoming dangerously slick with their sweat, although their act looked, from the ground, entirely effortless.

While the Mirnov Family was still flipping and swinging high above her, Olympia crept to the back of the tent where the other performers waited.

"You'll be wonderful," Ramus told her as he jumped in place to warm his muscles. He wore a black, formfitting bodysuit with a single shoulder strap and bound in the middle. He was barefoot and strong-browed and barrel-chested, and his legs were as thick as tree stumps; he looked a little like a clean-shaven caveman. Though hefty as a side of boiled beef, Ramus spoke with a gentle lisp. He had rubbed oil into his skin until it shone deep copper, as if he were made of some inflated and slightly flexible metal. He chalked his hands and glanced at Olympia genially.

Olympia opened her mouth to answer, to tell him that she was worried about the weeks that had passed since she'd last performed, to tell him she felt off-balance even on the ground, but she stopped when she was roughly slapped on the back.

"Luck! Luck! Luck!" Madame Barbue cried on her way through the crowd. Her beard was braided into two points with tiny ribbons tied at the ends—bright yellow to match the ribbons with which she'd tied her hair into two neatly twisted pigtails. She wore an enormous, lacy yellow dress, and her parasol was enormous, lacy and yellow, too; it dangled from her forearm on a wide yellow ribbon. Though she didn't perform in the main tent, she always made it a point to linger backstage there and keep the performers company while they readied themselves, and she clucked her well-wishes like a giant, fast-moving chicken, circulating among them, slapping backs and bottoms, and kissing cheeks, calling, "Luck! Luck! Luck!"

"You will be nothing but wonderful," Ramus told Olympia again. He smiled and flexed his chest to make the gold rings in his nipples jump and wink at her, just enough make her laugh.

IT WAS NOT UNTIL LATER that afternoon, in the middle of what was supposed to be time for the big top performers to rest while the barker lured the crowds into the sideshow tent, that Diamond struggled in.

Onstage, Minnie the Fat Lady, clad in what was essentially a large and colorful sack (this was only for the purpose of the show and was decidedly less extravagant and well-cut than her usual dress), sprawled on a small stool and slowly ate an enormous slice of cake as the audience jeered. Her knees, which Minnie ensured were in scandalously full view, peeped from under the hiked-up hem of her dress like pale brown dinner plates.

"Piggy!" a man in the audience—a man with a battered hat and sunken cheeks and horrible, tiny blue eyes, a man who looked as if he, too, had dressed himself very consciously as a sideshow character— yelled at the stage. "Piggy, piggy!" The rest of the crowd, catching on, began to call *Soooo-ee!* Minnie nodded and smiled and ate her cake, oblivious to the increasingly riotous audience. A woman threw a handful of hairpins at the stage and yelled, "Mulatto witch!" The pins clattered at Minnie's feet without effect, and she gave the furious woman a glowing smile and went back to eating her cake.

She knew—she'd explained it to Olympia—that in the poorer towns, like this one, merely sitting still with her cake and her pristine shoes and her ample body, she would rouse the audience to a fevered pitch and make a good show. She presented herself as the perfect picture of excess, a spoiled, greedy, and vapid woman, a willing steam valve to draw off the anger and frustration from folks who had nowhere else to put it. She'd grown up poor and brown-skinned in a mostly forgotten Creole neighborhood in Louisiana; she understood her job entirely too well. The more lavish her dress and the more she appeared to enjoy the cake, the fuller grew the bucket in which people dropped their pennies for the privilege of hurling insults at her and making her the object of their hate.

Olympia shrank into the background of the tent, nervously watching Minnie perform. The crowds scared her when they were riled like this, even though there were plenty of hands around (including Ramus) to quell any unruly troublemakers. She'd changed out of her spangled dress and wore a simpler one, cotton, drab in color, so that she might more easily slip among the crowds and not be recognized. Even so, she kept her head down, kept to the back of the tent, hid as best she could in plain sight.

The men and women in the crowd (children were not permitted entrance, and even the women were warned by the barker that some sights in the tent might be too much for them to abide without fainting) grew louder and angrier, shuffling and shouting at the stage. A scuffle broke out among a few of the men in the front row; about what they were arguing, nobody was quite sure, except that there were coin purses being waved about, and the men smelled of liquor and shoved each other without concern for gentility. Arms folded across his broad chest, Ramus stepped forward, followed by the other guardsmen, and sternly attempted to block the crowd from hurting Minnie despite the shouts and fists that had begun to be let loose. Minnie, for her part, tried to continue blithely eating her cake, but was clearly rattled, and ate more quickly than usual; the look on her face was more one of worry than of leering pleasure.

"The nerve," said a mousy woman beside Olympia. Her hair, her eyes, her dress were all dun; her skin was the quivering pale pink of a mouse's nose; she looked almost entirely, Olympia thought uncharitably, like an enlarged and angry mouse. "They should call her Fatty Antoinette," she said to everyone around her, clearly finding herself clever, "eating cake up there like a pig while the rest of us starve like dogs." She turned toward the stage, where Minnie continued to sit and eat, and yelled, "Let US eat cake, you black witch, you voodoo harlot!"

The woman was immediately ushered out on the arms of Ramus and one of the toughs who stood with him and she yelled loudly, until the rest of the crowd began to protest with her.

"Leave the lady alone!" a man yelled, though he did not dare step up to Ramus.

"They're hurting me!" the woman shrieked, and some of the men in the audience rushed toward her screams and stood aside only when Ramus extended one beefy red arm to press them back.

"We are just seeing the lady safely to the door," Ramus said gently and tried to clear a path as carefully as he could through the shoving, angry crowd.

Into this fray walked a woman, very pale and very blonde, taller and broader than most of the men in the crowd. She pulled behind her a battered steamer trunk, and her shoes were worn paper-thin and grayed with dirt. She pushed through the crowd until she reached the front seats and immediately attempted—strong and straight-armed with her open hand turned to the side, nothing like a lady should do when offering her hand—to shake the hand of Magnus Stephens, who owned the circus (which he half-jokingly called the "Magnusifent Review" among his employees but which, in public and officially, was called The Stephens Great Attraction)

Magnus, in his three-piece suit and gold watch chain, with his gray hair peppered with a bit of youthful black, his feet stuffed into very shiny shoes, looked exactly like what one would imagine a wealthy business owner should. The fact that he hid his hands under a gray silk kerchief in his lap (to obscure from view, Olympia knew, what more closely resembled a lobster's claws than human hands) drew absolutely no notice from the woman. When he didn't respond to her outstretched hand, but kept his own firmly hidden beneath their cover, the woman, never ceasing her speech longer than to brush away the sweaty strings of hair that had slipped from where they'd been pinned atop her head, simply shrugged and squatted next to his chair.

Minnie's performance was the last act in the sideshow, and after she'd finished her cake (hurriedly, nervously), the barker ushered the rest of the roiling crowd out of the tent and onto the dirt of the midway. Without looking in Olympia's direction, people shoved their way past her to the tent exit, though she hadn't faded again (she'd checked herself compulsively, as had become her habit in public, and was still quite solid and visible). The people smelled, as a crowd, awful—a combination of lilac perfume, sweat, and something acrid, like copper coins held too long in a sweating palm. Olympia shrank back to let them pass without brushing too closely against her.

At the front of the tent, nearest the stage, Magnus was bent low in conversation with the tall woman, who, since Magnus had obviously refused to stand and her legs were probably sore from squatting too long, had sat down on her trunk where she might look him in the eye more directly.

Although she'd not faded this time, still, no one saw Olympia as she stood at the back of the tent watching the stranger and Magnus deep in the throes of what appeared to be negotiation. When Olympia was not wearing the sparkling ribbons and lace of her costume, when she was not balanced precariously and courting a spotlight, when she was simply walking on solid ground and doing nothing of note, she could be any lost soul on the street. She was a plain woman, a faded brunette of average height and average build and slightly less-than-average beauty. When she was not performing, she drew no glance either of ire or admiration, absolutely no attention of any kind.

It was as if she wasn't there at all.

Two
The World's Smallest Man

HE WAS NOT ANYWHERE NEAR being the world's smallest man. In truth, Arnold was certainly small, but there were many well-documented cases of men and women shorter than he. However, he billed himself as The World's Smallest Major General (he was neither) Tiny Napoleon Only Three Feet Tall (he was four feet and change) and strutted about the stage in a semblance of a French naval commander's uniform. He barked at the crowd in a heavy French accent (on which he'd been schooled by Madame Barbue, so it was, in reality, a quite nasal Canadian French; he himself did not speak a word of French of any kind) and acted generally superior to the hoi polloi below. The crowds were usually so shocked at his performance (a man of his deficient stature, yet clearly so important and confident!) that nobody thought to question the fact that he was a whole thirteen inches taller than the broadsides claimed.

When he was not performing as Tiny Napoleon, Arnold was called Arnold. He cobbled shoes for all the performers, especially those in need of soft-soled, flexible shoes for acrobatic work. He was excellent at this job; he'd been apprenticed to a shoemaker as soon as his parents discovered that their son would never grow to a good, imposing, properly mannish height.

Arnold was notably small when he was born, though not alarmingly so, his parents thought. But as he grew older and, even well into his eighth year, was unable to help his father with his library because he could not reach above the third shelf of books without the use of a ladder no matter how hard he stretched, his parents began their worrying. The worry only grew as Arnold did not.

Despite this, Arnold himself was just fine, happy to read one of his father's many books in the library on the days when the sun was too hot to allow play outside. He particularly liked the books about science and those about foreign countries; he was not so fond of novels and books of poetry—those, he thought, were not pragmatic enough to be useful to a young and growing mind like his. What he wanted was real information, hard evidence of the world, stories of places and things that actually existed, not fantasy and rhyme. He was, down to his very toes, a pragmatist, excellent at mathematics and ledgers. He would, he assumed, become the bookkeeper for some small, but respected, establishment in a major city, wear a white shirt and tie to work, keep a townhouse and staff it with a humble group of servants, and marry an overripe woman who loved frivolous things, those things he eschewed, like music or painting, who loved them so passionately that she would burst into tears upon hearing a beautiful piece of music or upon reading a certain poem, even perhaps when wandering through their French-style gardens (she would insist upon the French style, riotous with color and barely controlled, plants spilling onto the garden paths, not the English style, composed, symmetrical, and properly manicured, as he preferred), and it would be left to him to caress her cheek, whisper softly, and bring her back to propriety.

When he was younger, Arnold had known a girl like this. Her name was Catherine, but she preferred to be called Magnolia because she had once seen the blossoms on a trip to her uncle's plantation in the south and found their odor absolutely exquisite. When she inquired after the name of the blooms, she found those syllables equally beautiful and took them for herself. She was, even by her own estimation, considerably less beautiful than the name warranted, but she had immense and persistent aspirations.

Magnolia lived with her parents, and Arnold frequently saw her strolling up the lane and stopping at the front garden of Arnold's house, bending daintily over the flowering bushes to sniff at them with obvious pleasure.

"Good morning, miss!" Arnold had finally screwed up the courage to say to her on one such occasion. He'd burst from his house as soon as he saw her (from his perch at the window where he was absolutely *not* waiting for her to pass, but simply enjoying the image of the sunlight dappling the yards).

"Why, hello!" Magnolia placed her hands on her knees and bent a bit in his direction, smiling widely. Arnold was used to this, as he was shorter than most people, and everyone assumed he was still a child. Magnolia held up her hand. Arnold, charmed to his core, took it immediately. The contact was buffered by the lace handkerchief that dangled from her sleeve; though he wished wildly to touch her bare hand, he dutifully allowed the kerchief to come between them. He kissed the hem of her sleeve and bowed low.

"Please take the liberty to call me Arnold, miss. I am exceedingly pleased to make your acquaintance," he said as formally as he could manage. "May I ask what name is beautiful enough to attach itself to such a creature?"

The girl giggled and drew her hand back quickly. "You are too kind, my dear little sir." She twirled one of her bright yellow corkscrew curls around her finger. "My name is Magnolia."

"Like the fragrant tree blossoms!" Arnold exclaimed.

Magnolia looked surprised that such a young man would know such a thing. "Why, yes!" she exclaimed. "Have you come from the south?"

"No, miss, I've lived here all my life. But I have read every book in my father's vast library," he said proudly. "Twice."

"You can read so well?" Magnolia looked properly impressed, her hand fluttering delicately to her chest, her eyes wide. "You're so young to be reading so much!"

Inside, Arnold bristled, but he would not let his face show it. "Not so young, miss. I'm twelve. It's just that I am small."

Magnolia looked horrified. "As old as I!" she gasped under her breath. Then she composed herself and smiled. "Not so small, and never you mind," she told him, looking as proud as if she'd just given him the most valuable jewel from her bosom.

"Thank you, miss," Arnold said and meant it.

After this meeting, Arnold waited at his window every day until Magnolia, parasol balanced primly on her shoulder, appeared on her walk. Upon seeing her, Arnold would hurry out the front door, attempting to appear as though he'd just rushed out to... smell that flower or... sweep the dirt from the walk with his foot. It was surely for some incredibly urgent reason and definitely *not* for the sole purpose of basking in Magnolia's presence, in any case.

"Arnold!" she would cry, as if she had not expected to see him, waving her lace handkerchief. And each time, Arnold would feign delighted surprise and offer his arm to walk her on his very own garden path.

They were great friends, perhaps even sweethearts, in this way for four years. Arnold walked Magnolia around his garden grounds every day without fail, unless it was raining, in which case the pair would sit in the overstuffed, heavily brocaded chairs in his father's library and pore over books about monkeys and elephants and the strange and wild flora of newly settled countries.

When they were sixteen, Magnolia began to talk about a man called Karl Schwinn, a cousin who'd come to live in America from Germany. Karl was a clockmaker who also collected clocks (which needn't be rare—it was the sheer number of clocks, rather than the quality of any of them, which interested him) and whose parlor was almost overbearingly loud with the ticking of hundreds of them. It drove Magnolia a bit mad, especially when she realized that all the clocks had been carefully synchronized to the second so that not a one made a tick when the others did not, so that the rhythmic clicking bored into her bones within a few minutes and caused her to speak in time with it. It made her feel like a mindless doll, and every second bit into the back of her mind with a nasty, stinging nip. To sit in that parlor was, she told Arnold, absolutely torturous to anyone with a mind and a will of her own.

She talked about Karl endlessly: his irritating clocks; his white-blonde hair, trimmed so short she could see the red of his scalp peeping through; the moustache he wore that was, oddly, an entirely different color from his hair (it was red); his irritating habit of greeting literally everyone on the street—even beggars—with a very formal bow and an inappropriately long and pointless conversation about the weather. Worst in Magnolia's eyes was Karl Schwinn's inability to properly knot his ties so that, instead of a neat knot at the base of his throat, the tie billowed just below his chin in a loose, flapping jumble which became progressively looser as he spoke and gestured in ardor until, by the end of the afternoon, it had come entirely undone and lay in two loose, limp strands against his shirt.

One afternoon, during their stroll through Arnold's gardens, Magnolia stopped to cup a wilting rose and looked at Arnold so plaintively that he could not help but ask, "What is it, Magnolia, that is troubling you?"

"Ah, me," she sighed, blinking back tears. It was one of the things Arnold loved about being friends with Magnolia, that the two of them could speak this way, as if they were the dashing and beautiful characters in the great romantic novels that Magnolia read (but Arnold absolutely would not, as those scribbles and heart-rendings were meant for sighing, frittering, vapid ladies and thus were completely beneath his intellect, though sometimes Magnolia and he sat together in his gardens and he listened raptly as she recounted for him in great detail the events of whichever novel she happened to be enjoying at the moment).

"I am afraid I must marry Karl, but I do not love him. Our families wish it, and he is completely taken with me. I find him dull, dear Arnold, and I do not want to be tied to a man so entirely devoted to me that he sees no one else."

Arnold nodded sagely and took this as a dire lesson. He, too, was completely devoted to Magnolia, but now he would never tell her so, as it would be the surest way to lose her affections irreparably. Instead of falling to his knees, professing his love, and begging her to run away with him, he held himself strong and simply put his hand lightly on the back of her wrist.

"What will you do? Will you run away?" he asked. Then, despite himself and full of hope, he added, "I can help you find your feet in a new town. We could flee to England as soon as a fortnight."

Magnolia smiled sadly at him. "Arnold, you are a dear to look after me this way, but I shall have to capitulate to the will of my family and Karl's ardent desires or be left penniless and without a family or home." She looked so pitifully at him that Arnold had to hold himself back from throwing her over his shoulder and leaping onto the nearest boat to take her away from her troubles and give her freedom.

"Besides," she added, "Karl is very rich."

The silence after that comment hung long and heavy between them. Arnold could give her many things—his keen intelligence, his knowledge of science and history, his utter devotion to her, his impeccable style and always properly tied ties—but he could not give her money, not right away, not if he left his family in scandal.

*   *   *

THIS WAS ARNOLD'S FIRST AND only broken heart. Once Magnolia had left to live with Karl on a rambling, be-gardened estate miles away ("Reader," she wrote to him in a looping, intricate script a couple of weeks later, "I married him"), Arnold was left quite alone. He realized then that he had neglected to befriend any other soul in favor of spending time with Magnolia, and, in her absence, no one was left to care for him.

In the wake of Magnolia, Arnold could not stir himself to find interest in any other girl. He resigned himself to a long and solitary life of study.

He would go to school, become a botanist, travel to newly discovered countries to catalogue the plant species there, and perhaps discover a new one (perhaps a flower, beautiful and fragrant, in a distant and unsettled jungle, which he would like to name after Magnolia, were her name not already given to another, previously discovered blossom). He spent long hours in his father's library, brooding over the books and moodily scribbling in his notebook drafts of letters to Magnolia which would never find shape and never be sent, and—against his family's express instructions—insisted on walking the gardens and showing himself in public (as if the neighbors did not whisper about him; as if he did not startle the kinder, older ladies at the market). It finally came to this: his parents had quite enough of the embarrassment of him and shipped him out to be apprenticed to a shoemaker.

He lived in the back of the shoemaker's shop like a horrible secret. The shoemaker, called Mister Wegg, was ashamed of Arnold's oddly disturbing shape, and would not let him talk with the customers for fear of losing them, though once when Arnold emerged from the workroom, a woman—after delicately shrieking in surprise—made the point that, being so close to the ground, Arnold was perhaps better suited to evaluating and repairing the damages to her shoes than anyone else. Even so, the shoemaker did not allow him to leave the workroom again, and so Arnold's bed was crammed into the corner there amid scraps of leather and iron awls and pilfered books and a small trunk of clothes, and he grew even paler from lack of sun. He stayed there, dutifully learning to cobble, until the day he decided to leave.

OLYMPIA FINALLY MET THE MYSTERIOUS new woman—who called herself Diamond—at the evening meal. She was seated next to Arnold at the long table, and the two of them were deep in animated conversation when Olympia sat across from them and smiled a shy hello.

"Miss Olympia Knife," Arnold said as he stood, "may I present to you Miss Diamond... er... Miss Diamond, what is your surname?" Diamond looked at him, stunned, and then hurriedly replied.

"Just Diamond. Diamond the Danger Eater, I think," she said, nodding firmly.

"But if you are Diamond the Danger Eater onstage," Arnold shook his head, "what is your real name?"

"Please." Her hand curled in a fist on the table. "I am Diamond."

Arnold smiled, bowed, and said, "May I present to you Diamond, the beautiful new jewel in the humble but golden crown that is The Stephens Great Attraction."

Arnold scuttled back into his seat, and Diamond winked and nodded at Olympia. "It's good to meet you," she said.

"Olympia is my real name, too," she said without thinking.

"Well, then, we can be nothing but the most authentic of friends," Diamond laughed easily, putting her hand atop Olympia's on the table. She winked again, then turned her attention to the stew in her bowl and things were quiet for a moment, save for the scrape of spoons and the endless chirping of the bugs at the tent entrance.

"Have you just joined us?" Olympia could not stop herself from asking. "Where have you come from? What can you do?"

Diamond gazed at her, and her eyes seemed to narrow and then soften again before she answered. She turned back to her stew, seeming to require a great deal of concentration to scrape up the next spoonful. "I come from Florida, not far away," she said mechanically. "I've just spoken with Mr. Magnus Stephens and I shall be staying on with the sideshow. I shall be called Diamond the Danger Eater, because I shall swallow swords and eat nails and glass."

"You can do that?" Olympia exclaimed in awe. She was, clearly, having a great deal of trouble keeping her own mouth under control.

But Diamond smiled widely, as if the question were not offensive at all. "Not yet. But I am a fast learner and I have an iron constitution."

"That's brave." It had been brave of Diamond to come to the Attraction on her own in the first place, Olympia thought. The confidence with which she seemed to do everything—go off on her own, deal with

Magnus, decide cheerfully to learn to do something so dangerous and unpleasant as swallowing glass—was overwhelming.

"Don't swallow any magnets, then," Olympia mumbled, but inside, she thought how strong, how confident and open this woman seemed. Inside, she thought, *But who will teach you?*

*   *   *

IT TURNED OUT THAT NOBODY taught Diamond to swallow swords, since nobody in all The Stephens Great Attraction knew how to do such a thing. So Diamond gamely and resolutely taught herself, as she usually did. She spent hours in the cruel heat of the main tent with her head pitched back to slowly accommodate her throat to the long ivory busk drawn from her corset. (Before she used an actual sword with a sharp point and blade, she began her attempts with the busk. This was helpful in two ways: Besides providing her a substitute, slightly more consumable, sword, it allowed her to free herself of the corset that would have made her work impossible). She learned by trial (the failures were disastrous and awful to watch, so, after an initial flurry of support and camaraderie from the other performers, Diamond practiced alone) to loosen her throat and tip her head to make her entire tract into one long column. Upon deciding that nails and glass were both too precious and too dangerous to work with, she resorted to the fairly easy feat of swallowing a chain, which she could pull back out of her body after taking it down her throat, and the lit end of a torch (this was more difficult, until she discovered the trick of keeping her cheeks full of enough water to douse it before damage occurred).

She refused, when it was suggested to her, to geek, because she could not bring herself to kill any living thing, much less bite its head off. But she did perform a trick in which she held several live mice— three, exactly—in her closed mouth before letting them spill back out free and alive (a trick which, she imagined with delight, might make the fainthearted in the audience shriek and jump up on their chairs, though the mice, having been carefully trained for just this trick, were never allowed to run free).

Once Diamond had practiced her stunts often enough that she could assure anyone watching they would not see her come to blood or harm, several performers offered to observe and give advice. The stunts were important, but just as important were the flourishes, the show she put on. Barbue and Ramus insisted that Olympia be brought in; as someone who had grown up in the circus, Olympia would be the best person to give advice about the choreography.

Olympia watched the act, and then instructed Diamond in a bit of showmanship: holding her arms wide, raising the sword or the fire or the mouse high in the air before slowly lowering the object into her open mouth (as if doing so required the utmost concentration and skill, which it sometimes did), and pausing, every once in a while, to heighten suspense as she went through the motions. Olympia was very good at these things.

"Turn your body so you don't face the crowd directly," she instructed, "like this," and without thinking, Olympia leapt to the stage and wrapped her hands around Diamond's waist to show her what she meant. The tiny chips of glass which covered Diamond's bodice (made to look like jewels, but far cheaper) pressed a little painfully against Olympia's fingers. Diamond smelled strongly of beeswax; her hair loosely brushed her bare shoulders; her waist was uncorseted and soft. Olympia dropped her hands as quickly as she'd allowed them to settle on Diamond's waist and looked away, blushing.

She was sure she'd faded again, but when Diamond cocked her head and looked directly at her with an unasked question, Olympia stammered.

"Like that," she said quickly, and leapt back off the stage to assume her seat.

Diamond turned her body, tipped her head back, lifted her arms with a flourish, and opened her mouth.

"*Exactement!*" shouted Madame Barbue, rising so fast she knocked her chair over.

"That's the way!" Ramus bellowed.

Diamond looked pleased and held a mouse, dangling by its tail, high over her face.

Olympia's stomach turned, but it wasn't because of the flailing, twisting white mouse. She could still feel the scratch of the cut glass studding that soft waist.

OLYMPIA RETIRED TO HER QUARTERS for the evening. She shared a trailer with Madame Barbue, but Madame had not yet come home, engaged as she probably was in some sort of collusive drinking with Ramus, as was often the case (she was a hard woman). Olympia sat alone on her bunk, trying to still her shaking hands but unable to stop thinking about Diamond, the hard-softness of her corseted waist, the beeswax smell of her. She tried to focus on mending the cotton leggings she wore under her high-wire outfit, because she already had a mother in Madame Barbue and felt disloyal and guilty whenever she thought of Diamond. Or perhaps it was not quite as a mother that she thought of her, and perhaps it was not quite disloyalty; Olympia wasn't sure. She felt, anyway, terribly wrong. She was thinking this way when she heard—almost didn't hear—a soft knock on the trailer door. She carefully laid the mending in the basket of ragged costume pieces and went to answer the door.

She found Diamond standing on the step with a bottle and two clinking glasses held aloft. Her white hair, her eyes, and her costume all sparkled delicately (and she really did look, in the darkness and the moonlight, like a handful of diamonds glittering from the bottom of a well), but her movements were firm and sure. Diamond cocked her head and waggled the glasses. "You ran out, and I didn't thank you for the help. The show works much better now. Thanks for the advice."

"Okay," said Olympia, not moving.

"May I?" Diamond asked, pressing Olympia aside with a hip.

Olympia shifted to let Diamond in. "I guess you may, then."

Diamond handed Olympia the glasses and used her now-free hand as a brace against the doorframe to heft herself into the trailer. Olympia may have been exceptionally limber, but even at her most charitable, she recognized that Diamond was rather clumsy. This was probably in part because she was so tall; when they stood facing each other, as they did now, the tip of Olympia's nose came just level with Diamond's shoulder.

"Arnold gave me the glasses and the gin," said Diamond, settling herself on the doily-covered divan and opening the bottle. "He told me to bring it to you, but not to mention it had come from him. I think he thought it would help lubricate my apology."

"Arnold is a busybody." Olympia took one of the glasses. She sipped lightly, as her constitution had never permitted much alcohol, and the gin smelled so strongly of juniper she felt as if she were licking a pine tree.

"Cheers, Arnold," Diamond said, raising her glass. Olympia did the same, and they knocked them together before drinking.

Though he was typically rather crusty and kept to himself, Arnold had never been anything but kind and fatherly to Olympia. In her mind, in secret, she used to match him with Minnie, who had never been anything but kind and motherly to her. The two of them were so often paired in the sideshow, Arnold being so short and Minnie being so fat, that Olympia easily imagined them as her own parents. Or, perhaps because she did not want to forget her own missing father and mother, she pictured Arnold and Minnie as her fairy godparents, slightly unreal, mismatched, loving her without question or limit.

Diamond shoved herself a little farther back onto the cot and splashed more gin into her glass. She winced as she moved, until she had successfully slumped into a comfortable position (the glass on her costume, Olympia assumed, was the reason for most of the discomfort). Her long, thick legs, gangly in mauve stockings, draped from the cot and onto the floor. She was pale and glittering, hard and soft all at once; she was, Olympia thought, not exactly beautiful, but compelling.

Olympia told Diamond Arnold's story—or, at least, what bits of it she knew—and Diamond performed a very good approximation of Arnold's soft, overblown speech, punctuating every phrase with *Madame* and *if you please*. They whispered and laughed lightly, heads bent together and cheeks nearly touching, feeling themselves absolutely alone in Olympia's cot and easily forgetting about Madame Barbue's neatly made bed mere feet away and the imminent presence it suggested. Though Olympia pressed, Diamond refused to speak about her own past any further than to say she was from Florida, and had left her home because she'd seen the circus come into town, and had felt called away from her repetitive, all-too-still life.

When Olympia asked what home she'd left behind, Diamond shook her head. "It was so long ago," she said, though it had been less than a week since her arrival. "I couldn't launder the napkins or beat the rugs even one more time, and they needed me far too desperately; I thought I might go crazy."

This was all she would say.

Between the two of them, the bottle was lightened by three more glasses, and the women grew rosy and giggly. Diamond's headband slipped low, almost covering her eyes, and she splayed, sloppy and loose, across the blanket. She was, Olympia thought, quite unintentionally beautiful.

When Diamond hiccupped and threw her arms around Olympia's shoulders and whispered, *"I'm so glad I ran away!"*, Olympia's hands went cold, and she felt a shock of weakness travel down both arms, but nothing—no explanation, no story, and certainly no sweet kiss on the mouth—followed the revelation. There was only the sound of Diamond softly breathing and the weight of her head on Olympia's shoulder; Diamond seemed to fill the space entirely. Her hair—white, shining—spilled over Olympia's shoulder. The smell of beeswax and juniper was everywhere. Though Olympia was hot and dizzy, she stayed as still as she could so as not to disturb Diamond's position.

It was as though Arnold had planned this, Olympia thought, as though he had been sure that Olympia would be this utterly spellbound, that she would feel this happy and this terrified at the same time. (Although he was a bit officious, Arnold was also rarely wrong.) She lay perfectly still, but Olympia's heart raced and she couldn't catch a deep breath, and she swelled with everything—happiness, fear—she'd worked hard all her life to keep at bay. For more than an hour, she stared at her own hand on Diamond's hip and waited for the sight of it to fade, but nothing happened. Lying there with Diamond half-drunk and sleeping on her shoulder, Olympia remained, for as long as she kept herself awake, bloomingly happy and solid.

SOMEONE POUNDED ON THE DOOR of the trailer, shouting for Olympia to come out and help them search. For what, she didn't know, but she sat bolt upright, her heart banging, suddenly sober. Diamond startled awake only a moment before Madame Barbue burst through the door with her usually neatly tied hair wild and slipping sideways.

"Olympia, my heart, you must come help us immediately. Everyone is searching, Minnie is beside herself," she cried.

"What? Who?" Olympia had jumped to her feet and tossed a wool shawl around her shoulders before she'd even thought to ask the questions. Diamond, for her part, was pressing her hair back into shape and looking frantic.

"It's Monsieur Arnold! Like your parents! Right in front of Monsieur Ramus! He went into his trailer while Monsieur Ramus was waiting outside, but never came out again, and now it's empty!"

Olympia struggled to calm her heart and gather herself. Arnold, who was generally gruff and unpleasant, could not restrain himself from spoiling Olympia. He had guarded her and soothed her and tutored her in all matters of geography and culture and history, had absolutely no willpower when it came to resisting her tantrums or pleading and, at least according to Barbue, indulged the child far too frequently.

For a time just after her parents had disappeared, Olympia even began to call him Papa, until Arnold sternly told her that he was not her father, and she could not disrespect the memory of Alban Knife that way. Olympia had cried silently into Minnie's lap for a long hour, until Arnold relented and apologized to her, and he and Minnie together had explained the situation more carefully. Still, in her head, she imagined him as Papa, though she would never again say it out loud.

Now Arnold was missing and Olympia was twice fatherless, but she would not let herself weaken into tears in front of Barbue and Diamond. Madame Barbue seemed, for her part, completely unconcerned with looking weak, having worked herself into such a frenzied state that she was rushing about the room, frantically picking up objects (a comb, a bottle) and putting them back down in a pantomime of useless, frenetic energy.

"What?" Diamond asked, rubbing her eyes. "What's happening? Has something happened?"

Madame Barbue turned to Diamond, grabbed her shoulders, and shook until the beads on her costume rattled.

"Arnold has vanished."

Three
The Rubber Boy

WHEN HE WAS BORN, HIS parents gave him the good Christian name of Daniel, which is actually a good Hebrew name meaning "God is my judge." This turned out to be less than true, because it seemed as though everyone—including, but not limited to, God—was Daniel's judge.

Daniel, in the Old Testament Bible, was a prophet who rose in the king's court by interpreting dreams, and Daniel's parents knew this as well. They also knew the old stories about a child born with a caul over his or her eyes. Daniel was born with such a caul, exactly as the old wisdom spoke of, looking very much like a plucked and undercooked chicken with a lacy membrane spread over his face that his parents were afraid to touch. Because of this, his mother and his father both (not to mention their parents and grandparents) were convinced that Daniel had been given the gift of second sight.

This turned out to be exactly true.

As a baby, Daniel would begin to cry long before a storm settled over the family's Virginia farmland. He cried just before his father left the house each morning and in the moments just before they discovered that a cow had gone missing or a chicken had died. He would cry when food was scarce, as if he knew the hardship the family suffered. He would cry just before a meal was served, as if he were weeping at the evidence of God's great bounty. He cried before rain, knowing how frightening the pounding on the roof would become, and he cried before drought, understanding even then the dangers it brought their farm. He cried, and he cried, at almost everything. But his exhausted mother and father knew his cries were more than simply the insistent screeches they seemed to be; those cries were, his parents knew, portentous, though what they were meant to portend only made sense in the aftermath, when the cries could be properly interpreted and understood in light of the facts (his father said this was true of the dreams of many seers as well). So Daniel's mother and father protected him and heeded his yowling and held him up as a very special Gift to their family.

Daniel was pale, tall, and far too thin. As he grew into a young man, he showed himself to be neither particularly strong, nor particularly smart, nor particularly skilled at anything useful, but he had been made particularly comfortable with his mother and father, who expected little and praised him greatly for much less. Daniel simply *was*, though he could be said to *be* no particular thing at all, and he fit into and around the lives of everyone he loved, quietly, easily, and unmemorable.

When he was eleven years old, Daniel's parents took him to see the Reverend Joseph Small, who had been permitted to set up camp in a yellow- and white-striped tent on Jacob Roberts's land, just at the river's edge, where a clearing had been cut in the trees and the ground was smooth enough for a tent to stand. In exchange for the land and two meals a day, the Reverend Joseph Small had agreed to bless the Roberts family, the farm, and each of the animals there. Daniel's parents presented him, with a short summary of his gifts, to the Reverend Small after one of the revivals. The Reverend Small was sweaty and exhausted and as red as a cooked lobster, but he agreed to sit with Daniel and his parents and hear what they had to say.

"Do you think there is a place for our Daniel in your ministry?" Daniel's father asked hopefully, after they had explained Daniel's abilities fully and to their own satisfaction.

The reverend shook his head. "No, sir, I am sorry, but we have no place for Daniel here."

"But why?" Daniel's father exclaimed, rising halfway out of his seat. "He has a Gift from God! Surely you will want such a shining example—"

"He has a gift from the Devil," the reverend interrupted.

Daniel's mother stood to leave. She took Daniel's arm in hers as she did. Daniel's father grabbed her skirt and pulled, firmly saying, "No. Sit." She did, and pushed Daniel into his chair. Daniel, for his part, sat absolutely quietly, trying to look every bit like a boy who was not given a gift by the Devil.

"This is no Devil's gift," his father spat at the Reverend Small. "He can see what will come to be, just like the prophets in the Bible."

The Reverend Small withdrew a very white kerchief from his breast pocket and mopped his forehead, sighing heavily, as if it pained him to explain this simple situation to these stubborn and willfully ignorant folk. "The time of the Bible has long passed," he said. "God no longer gives such gifts. What makes you think that your boy is special enough in God's eyes to receive such a prize over the rest of us good souls? Daniel, do you do the Lord's work?"

"He does indeed!" his father said, firmly squeezing Daniel's shoulder.

"I have asked Daniel," the Revered Small said evenly. "Daniel, is this the work you were born to do? Do you do it in the Lord's name and for the benefit of God?"

Daniel looked terrified, as he was unused to being asked to speak. "I don't know, sir," he said. "I obey my parents in all things, but sometimes I see visions, and I can neither control nor understand them." It was true that, on occasion, the lights of angels flashed so brightly in his head he couldn't see or hear anything else. He made a disturbing sight at those moments, with his body gone slack and useless and his eyes rolled back in his head. The visions were dramatic, but nothing ever came of them—no messages, no understanding, no portent—and nobody could properly interpret them (least of all Daniel himself) until it was too late.

"My visions come over me without warning or will. They cause me fits and they don't make a bit of sense. I could not do it in the Lord's name if I wished, since I can't seem to control it at all." Daniel's father's hand tightened on his shoulder like a sharp vise. "But I do wish it be for the Lord," Daniel added hastily.

The Reverend Small sighed and wiped his forehead again with the bright white hankie. "I see, Daniel, you are a good boy. But your body is being used by the Devil for his own purposes, and you must resist it." He turned to Daniel's mother and father. "This is vanity, if you think it is a gift from God. This is pride. God does not give such gifts to his servants. Humble yourselves. Have you ever met a single person with such powers in your natural life?" The reverend shook his head, and despite himself, Daniel's father shook his own head in agreement. "I have traveled for years, and I have met no such man." The Reverend Small stood and turned to leave the tent, still shaking his head.

"You're meeting him now!" Daniel's mother cried. She jumped from her seat, yanked Daniel onto his feet, and pushed him toward the reverend, who reared back as if to touch Daniel would be to touch the Devil himself.

"I am truly sorry, madam, sir, but I cannot help you." The Reverend Small turned on his heel and left.

As THEY WALKED THE THREE miles home along the muddy riverbank, Daniel's parents hissed an argument. Each of them held one of Daniel's arms, and he was nearly dragged along between them as they walked.

"I told you, Caroline, that we should not bother the good reverend with this. Our boy is nothing special, and now, when word of this spreads, that the world-famous Reverend Joseph Small has turned him away, people will begin to talk badly."

"People already talk badly!" his mother cried, jerking Daniel's arm so that he stumbled closer to her. "People talk badly because you do not go to church every Sunday and they wonder what you are doing that is more important! People talk badly because you insist on wearing a silk vest and tie into town, even though you work in a field and your wife's own shoes are cracked and worn!" Daniel's father had yanked his arm to pull him closer while his mother shouted, and now, his mother yanked again to pull him back to her side. Daniel felt exhausted and let himself be pulled along. He was used to being the bridge between them.

"You have nothing but the finest things!" his father growled and pulled Daniel back to his side.

"*Daniel* has nothing but the finest things!" His mother stopped short and glared directly at Daniel. Her fingers tweaked the collar of the new, bright yellow velveteen jacket into which they'd forced him that morning. "His own mother lives in near squalor!" She lifted her satin boot, covered in the mud of the riverbank, as evidence. Daniel's father scoffed, though the vision of the muddy shoes seemed to take him aback.

"Take him, then. He is yours to school and yours to comfort when he cries. He knowingly ruined our chances with the Reverend Small, probably because you willed it!"

"I did no such thing!" his father shouted, pushing Daniel back toward his mother. Daniel stumbled, and his knee hit the mud. He stood as quickly as he could, brushing his legs desperately.

"You see?" his mother cried, "Your own wife is hobbling about in broken, filthy shoes while your son ruins his expensive trousers!"

"You spoil him so that he has no appreciation of God or the things we work hard for!"

"He does not work at all!" His mother pushed him back toward his father. "You allow him to sit like a wilting rose, scribbling his drawings in the shade while you tend the animals yourself! You work in the field, and I am near to a scullery maid in the house, and our son imagines he is an *artiste!*" She hissed the word in Daniel's direction with all the venom she seemed able to muster (which was, Daniel noted, quite a bit).

"At least I have tried to show him how real work is done!" His father's voice was growing hoarse from yelling. "You sit in the house, embroidering flowers onto the cushions, while I toil outside!"

"Your field hands toil while you stand by and watch!"

"I toil as well! I do so toil as well!"

His father gave Daniel one last great shove, and Daniel stumbled a few steps into the river. His parents, still arguing, continued walking and shouting, and did not notice that Daniel was no longer between them.

As his parents stormed onward, Daniel stood in the water and watched. He did not move, but preferred to stay there, waiting, to find out how long it would take them to discover his absence. The water slap-splashed past his legs, seeped, ice cold and muddy, into his shoes, and climbed up the legs of his trousers all the way to his belt.

He stood for what seemed like hours before he realized his parents were not coming back.

DANIEL FOLLOWED THE RIVER UNTIL the sky was black and lit only by stars. He did not see a soul, and his parents didn't come looking for him. He was not sure they'd yet noticed he was gone. (Perhaps they had. Perhaps it didn't matter.) When he was too exhausted to walk farther, he crawled up the bank of the river until he found a spot between two trees, spongy with fallen leaves, and he slept there.

The next day, as soon as the sun began to brighten the sky, Daniel was up. He walked until he found a road—stopping to steal an apple from an orchard, but only one small apple, and he left a penny on the fence post, because he did *not* have a gift from the Devil and refused to act as if he did—and then he walked some more. A passing carriage stopped, and the man driving—whom he'd never seen, though he'd lived in these parts all his life—allowed him to ride in the wagon, where he did his best to cling to the sides as it jolted loosely down the rutted road, continually tossing its contents of hay bales, a cord of chopped wood, two lanky dogs, and Daniel.

When they reached the town, Daniel jumped off, waved his thanks to the wagon driver, and began to walk again. When he found the circus tents pitched near the edge of town, he stopped.

IT HAD BEEN LESS THAN a day, but he felt as though he hadn't eaten in weeks and ravenously sucked down the soup and bread that was given to him by the cooks in the big tent. As payment, they put him to work hoisting tent poles and heavy rolls of canvas from the wagons where they were stored and digging holes in the ground where the tent poles would be steadied. They gave him a place to wash and then to sleep (he was allotted a bed in a trailer already packed with three other men), and, in the morning, he was given breakfast and ushered out to erect the smaller tents. Nobody asked if he would like to work and travel with them; everyone just assumed Daniel would remain.

After a few weeks, Daniel had come to be friends with a handful of the crew, who roughly but fondly knocked his shoulders when they greeted him. Like all folks working in The Stephens Great Attraction, he was given a new name. The crew began to call him Robin, and it caught on amongst the entire circus, until he was no longer ever referred to as Daniel, thought of himself only as Robin, and was introduced that way to everyone who met him. And one day, he realized, Daniel had ceased entirely to exist.

They called him Robin because he whistled while they worked and, on meal breaks, he entertained the entire lot by jumping onto the table to do his impressions of members of the crew, Mr. Stephens himself, the elephants and the monkeys, famous stage actors and, most notably, birds. He could be, they said, anyone or anything. And so, because his birdcalls were so convincing that even the animals in their cages perked up their ears when he whistled, he was given the name of the cheerful harbinger of springtime, the name he'd keep for the rest of his life.

He worked on the crew as they erected and struck the tents in the hot sun every week in a new location and earned a special place among the workers not for his strength (he was wiry, and of average power at best, perhaps even a little weaker than most), but for his flexibility. He could crawl into the tightest space to reach a lost rope or stretch farther than anyone to snag a loose tent corner. So it came as no surprise when, one day, Magnus approached him, with Ramus at his side, to ask if he would like to become Robin the Rubber Boy.

They had an idea for an act in which Robin might display his extraordinary flexibility, an act that would require no hoax or mirrors, and Robin agreed. He developed a performance in which he folded himself to fit into the tiniest carpet bag, and stretched his earlobes by putting hooks through them and suspending there the smallest of the trained dogs, or, in their absence, the snakes of the snake charmer Harem Harriet.

He bent his arms and legs in disturbing ways that appeared to dislocate the joints but, at the end of the act, Robin snapped back, triumphantly, into shape.

*   *   *

EVER SINCE THE NIGHT DIAMOND fell drunkenly asleep on Olympia's shoulder, she had seemed to avoid Olympia. After each of her performances as the Danger Eater (which became wildly popular), she retired immediately to her trailer. She practiced alone, in secret, at night, long after everyone had gone to sleep. She roomed with Minnie, and they entertained, occasionally, Madame Barbue; from behind the tightly closed doors and windows, one could hear Diamond's and Minnie's monotone babble and, glittering above it, Madame Barbue's laughter.

Olympia settled back into being by herself and only a little bit lonely. She spent her days with Minnie, bent over a basket of mending, and alone on the wire she'd had the crew stretch across two posts in the yard for her practicing; she learned to hurl herself into a midair flip and land, balanced precisely, back on the wire. Staying visible took more and more of her concentration; her natural state, when she let her vigilance rest, was translucence, only half there. Often, when mending costumes with Minnie or eating dinner with the rest of the family, Olympia would shimmer and filter halfway gone, like dust in sunlight, and the others would pat her arm and tell her to stick around, reminding her to stay calm, think happy thoughts. When she walked the wire, then, she had to spend so much of her effort focusing on just staying solid that she often neglected her balance and missed a step or nearly fell.

On occasion, she strolled into town (alone, or on the arm of one circus man or another) to browse the bolts of cotton at the local dry goods store. On one such afternoon, she went with Walter, a dashing and well-muscled man who worked on the crew as a rigger and spent his free time on the midway, drunkenly trying, with the other young men, to ring the bell at the strength-testing booth, even though they knew it was rigged so that only an impossible feat of human strength would move the iron marker above sixty (which was labeled, mockingly, ARE YOU SURE? on the machine). Walter kindly smoothed her hand over his arm and escorted her into the dry goods store, where he promptly disappeared to the room behind the counter with the storeowner and a suspicious-looking flask he pulled from his vest.

Olympia looked at the small stack of calico and plain woven cotton behind the counter, hoping to find something with which she might spruce up an old dress and make it new again. She browsed only halfheartedly, for she really didn't care about the cottons at all and was, instead, drawn to watch what seemed to be a growing ruckus outside the store, on the street. A crowd of men and women had gathered around something she couldn't see, though she could easily tell they were furious and shouting.

She left the store, slipped into the crowd, and pushed her way through it until she could make out, at its center, the object of everyone's attention. It was Diamond, alone and looking terrified, as a squat and furious woman—so stooped she was even shorter than Olympia, and only reached just above Diamond's waist—screamed.

"Thief! Where do you have it? Dirty thief!"

A man with the white shirt and green visor of a banker, who clearly prided himself on his control and reason, pushed between the two women.

"What's the trouble here?"

"She was in my store, and I saw her steal fifty cents and an apple! I saw it!" the woman screamed.

The man turned to Diamond. "Miss, I'd advise you to give back what rightfully belongs to Mrs. Bursley here." He gestured and bowed toward the woman in question, who huffed and nodded and folded her arms across the front of her dress.

"Indeed!" Mrs. Bursley said.

Diamond looked terrified, though she towered above nearly everyone gathered there and was certainly much taller than the squat, screeching old bat accusing her.

"I took nothing," she said. "I was only looking at the apples. I have no money."

"If you have no money for buying apples," Mrs. Bursley said, as if she'd caught Diamond in the cleverest trap, "then why were you looking at the apples in my store, hmm?" She turned to address the crowd. "She's from that traveling show, The Greatest Stephens What-all, the circus, and you know the kind of woman…" Mrs. Bursley let her voice trail off suggestively.

A ripple of muttering went through the crowd, muttering which increased in volume when Diamond said again, "I was only looking at the apples."

"Search her, you'll find it! She has my money, too, the gargantuan beast!" Mrs. Bursley spat, and the men in the crowd looked uncertainly at Diamond until Mrs. Bursley cried again, "Are you afraid? Search her, I said!"

One of the men swiped the hat from his balding head and lowered his eyes as he approached Diamond, hands already reaching. "I'm sorry, ma'am, I must do this."

Diamond looked wildly through the crowd, but no man there seemed interested in doing anything but watching the show. "Please," she said, "Leave me." No one paid mind to her. Some of the men averted their eyes, clearly ashamed, yet unable to turn away completely from what was sure to be a salacious scene.

"Stop!" Olympia cried, and the crowd turned to see who had yelled. Even Mrs. Bursley froze.

"They're in league!" Mrs. Bursley broke the moment of silence. "I saw them whispering together on my porch!"

Olympia froze, stunned at the depth of the lie. Everyone else stopped talking upon seeing Olympia's stunned face. Diamond seized the opportunity; she raised her fist and brought it down squarely on the shoulder of the balding man, then turned and ran.

Olympia ran after her, calling, "Diamond! Wait!" but Diamond would not stop. Though her legs were considerably longer than Olympia's, she was far less nimble, and Olympia easily overtook her. She grabbed Diamond's arm and pulled her along until the two reached the river, where they hid in the cover of trees, breathing hard, until they were quite sure nobody was looking for them any longer. (Olympia was fairly certain nobody had been chasing them in the first place, but she kept that detail to herself.)

"I thought they would kill me," Diamond whispered.

Olympia gave a breathless laugh. "That gnome only wanted to touch you," she said bitterly. "And the others only wanted to watch."

"And that woman—" Diamond tried to add.

"Wanted to see them do it, because she's a nasty little witch who's forgotten what it's like to be a girl on her own."

"We don't know that," Diamond tried charitably.

"We don't care, either," Olympia said, and Diamond laughed.

Olympia still held Diamond's hand and pulled her to sit in the dirt at the base of a tree. She leaned her shoulder against the trunk and looked at Diamond.

"Are you all right?"

Diamond nodded. "That was a horrible scene. I wouldn't like to repeat it, and I won't be going into town again—at least not by myself— for a very long time."

"I'll take you," Olympia said, though she was so much smaller than Diamond that the idea that she would be her protector was ridiculous, like the thought of a puppy walking its master.

"I'm not sure that would make much difference," Diamond said. "Two girls alone, and you're so small—"

"I got you out of there this time, didn't I?" Olympia asked. "It was just us two girls this time. And you really gave it to that guy. I think you can handle yourself, even alone."

Diamond laughed. "I did knock him pretty hard."

"He's going to be awfully sore, when he's able to move his arm again," Olympia said. She still held Diamond's hand, as she had when they ran. Her grip was sweaty and tight, and Olympia knew she had held her hand long past the moment when it made sense, but Diamond didn't seem inclined to let go either. Olympia squeezed and knocked their hands against her thigh, just to acknowledge they were still connected.

Diamond raised her eyebrows and looked at her, squeezing back.

So Olympia did the most natural thing she could think of: She lifted their hands and pressed her lips to the back of Diamond's wrist. She even, in quite a gallant manner, held her lips there and looked up very deliberately at Diamond, inviting a response, as she'd seen men do so many times.

"My," whispered Diamond, sliding her hand away. She stood, smoothed her skirt, and would not meet Olympia's eyes. "We should get back to the tents," she said, but didn't move.

"Yes," Olympia blushed. "It's getting late, and you have a show this evening."

"Yes," whispered Diamond mechanically. "I do."

And then, despite all the very clear messages warning her against such behavior, Olympia put her hand on Diamond's cheek and kissed her lightly on the mouth.

Diamond, without a word, stood and smiled sadly, then held out her hand to help Olympia up.

WHEN THEY RETURNED, THE LONG table in the gathering tent was just being laid for dinner.

"You nearly missed everything," Robin said.

"It's true," Olympia said in a monotone. "I was in town."

"What did you do?" Robin scrubbed the table with a rag, then laid the tin plates and cups gently in a row of settings down its length. Olympia couldn't answer, but only heard the echo of the question in her head: *What did you do? What did you do?*

"She went to buy fabric for her dresses," Diamond said. "And then she rescued me."

Olympia nodded. Robin scrubbed, looking dubious.

"A little old witch accused me of stealing," Diamond said, "and a bunch of fellows were crowding me on the street, and Olympia distracted them long enough for us to get away."

"Good grief," said Robin with a wowed descending whistle. "Are you all right?"

"She punched a man," Olympia blurted, and both Diamond and Robin looked at her.

"You punched a fellow?"

"I did," Diamond said.

"You probably shouldn't go into town alone now," Robin said. "Maybe not at all."

"I wasn't planning on it. Besides, the show will leave this rotten town in less than a week."

Robin turned to place a napkin on each chair seat, as if the matter had been resolved and nothing more about it interested him. Olympia stood awkwardly. Diamond raised her eyebrows and looked at her meaningfully over Robin's back.

"I need to go." Olympia pointed over her shoulder toward the trailers.

"Wait," Diamond said, at the same time that Robin said, "Are you all right?"

Olympia kept walking. If she stayed, she knew, she wouldn't eat a single bite anyway.

* * *

THE NEXT DAY WAS THE final show in that town, and one of the hottest, most awful afternoons Olympia could remember. She was, however, relieved: After today, the entire circus would spend Sunday striking the tents and the equipment; then they would pack their wagons, board up the animals, and head to the next swampy town, where nobody knew them and she could start fresh. All of it would be gone—kissing Diamond; her soft waist underneath the makeshift sequins of rough glass; the way Diamond had pulled back, looking frightened, but still silently held Olympia's hand on the long and humiliating walk back to the tents. All of that would be left far behind them, and Olympia could start anew.

As she usually did, Olympia snuck across the midway and into the freak show to watch the variety acts before she had to walk the tightrope in the main tent. The crowds were large and rowdy and sweaty, catcalling and shoving their way down the midway and into the sideshow tent. It was an ugly Saturday, humid and hot, and the June beetles, big and meaty as fists, slammed themselves against fence posts and tent sides in ugly suicide runs, leaving a fine coat of sun-warmed slime over everything. Minnie's show was a disaster, and she had to be escorted off the stage by two of the biggest crewmen to ensure that none of the heat-crazed and furious folk in the audience did as much violence as they threatened.

After the last mess with Minnie's show, they'd changed the order of the performances. Now, Robin's act was the final one, and a good one to follow Minnie: He stirred in his audience only horrified pity, because he was exceedingly, skeletally thin, and because the poorer folks in the audience (which comprised, in that place, most of the audience) considered him to be a less fortunate version of themselves and immediately sympathized. The ways in which he contorted and stretched his own body looked painful, and pain was something to which many of them could relate.

Robin knew this and emphasized this aspect of his act, going so far as to groan and twist his face in a grotesque rictus of agony when— Olympia knew—he felt no such thing. This was a detail that mattered little, because he *appeared* to suffer, and even this indirect identification with the audience was good enough.

After he had bent and stretched and contorted himself beyond what anyone watching imagined he might, Robin stepped gingerly into a small trunk, then carefully folded himself smaller and smaller, until he fit entirely into the case, and a cowering woman chosen from the audience closed the lid, sealing him inside. The stage lights dimmed, and a drum rattled to heighten the suspense. The woman who'd closed the trunk covered her own mouth with her hands and stepped back into the shadows of the stage; one of the beefiest stage crew held her arm so she wouldn't fall if she fainted. Everyone waited. Olympia counted to five, at which time she knew Robin would burst out of the trunk, unfold himself, and throw his hands victoriously over his head while the audience roared its approval.

Olympia counted, and nothing happened. She counted again, this time to ten, and still nothing happened. The drum rattled a moment longer, then fell silent. The audience began to mumble. Something had gone wrong.

Two of the crew rushed onto the stage to pry at the lid of the trunk, which fell open to reveal—and here Olympia gasped along with the rubes—an entirely empty box.

Whispers of shock and interest hissed around her from the crowd. Madame Barbue, who had been watching from just offstage, wailed and rushed to examine the box. Olympia joined her, along with several other performers, and even some of the braver men in the audience. Nothing was there.

"Robin!" Madame Barbue shrieked, swiping the inside of the trunk with both arms, as if he might be hiding there, in one of the box's corners, somehow as yet unseen. "He's disappeared!"

The hissing crowd grew louder as they began to realize this drama was not part of the show. The hissing broke into wails and one woman, squeezed too tightly among people pushing down the aisles to get out of the tent, fainted in her tracks. She was immediately surrounded by half the crowd, by people slapping her hands and calling gently to revive her, while the rest of the audience ran from the tent in panic.

Onstage, a small group of performers gathered to console Madame Barbue, who was now hysterically weeping and pulling at her beard like a hired mourner. None of the audience was paying them attention; the little stage felt like a private room.

"*Mon petit oiseau!*" she cried, and Olympia took her into her arms.

The men in the crew glanced sideways at Madame Barbue; the hysteria made them nervous. Instead of consoling her, they took charge, all of them, barking orders that nobody followed, pushing each other aside as they all searched for Robin, and thoroughly examining the empty trunk, the stage itself, the curtains, even the poles that held them up. Minnie went so far as to crawl, peering, under the chairs, calling, "Robin, boy! Come out! Show's done for!"

The longer they searched, the darker the sky became and the more hopeless their efforts seemed. Minnie, tears in her eyes, finally whispered good night to them all and slunk off to her trailer, where she would seal herself inside to cry so nobody could see her and emerge in the morning newly steeled and contained. Olympia held Madame Barbue and rocked her gently, as Barbue herself had done for Olympia on so many nights after her parents had disappeared. Madame Barbue, sufficiently exhausted and despondent, finally quieted her wailing to a soft hiccup. One by one, the searchers gave up and left the tent to go drink themselves to sleep. Once only Ramus, Barbue, and Olympia remained, Ramus stood, placed his hand gently on Madame Barbue's shoulder, and bent to kiss her forehead.

"Good night, Madame," he whispered. "Don't worry. Robin will turn up, and we will all have a good laugh at his trick. It will all be fine in the morning." He stood, extinguished the last light, and left Madame Barbue clinging to Olympia and quietly snuffling on the empty stage.

They waited long into the night, but Robin did not turn up. Eventually, the two women, wrung-out as wet bedsheets, fell asleep in a heap, their arms still clasped around each other, on the floor of the stage in the lightless tent.

Robin was nowhere to be found.

Four
The World's Wealthiest Lobster

WHEN THE WOMEN WOKE THE next morning, Robin had not returned. By that evening, there was still no sign of him. When another day had passed without any hint of him, Madame Barbue and Olympia and the entire crew gave up on ever seeing him again.

Madame Barbue became useless; she wore the same dress—her yellow one, meant only for the stage—every day for a week. She did not bathe—her hair was matted and her beard was snarled without the careful braiding and ribbons—and she stank, an awful combination of liquor and sweat and dirt. She spent the daylight hours locked alone in her trailer, weeping. At night, she ventured out to drink herself stupid on the steps of her home and would throw her glass of whiskey at anyone who dared speak to her. Olympia only entered the trailer when she absolutely had to do so—the depth of Barbue's grief was too difficult to abide—and then only after the woman had passed out in her bunk. Olympia left full glasses of water by her bedside and little gifts (a handful of sweet clover flowers, a kind note) on her chair, but preferred to stay far away from Barbue's grief and spent her free time mending costumes with Minnie in the shade of the gathering tent. Everyone crept past the trailer as if Madame Barbue's quiet were tenuous and fragile, as if the very noise of their feet on the gravel would break the peace wide open and her howling would start again, as loud as if it had never stopped.

Olympia and some of the crew took over Madame Barbue's chores—cooking the stew, washing the dishes—and the rest of the variety show members compensated to cover her missing act, so that Magnus Stephens would not notice her absence from her duties. After several days, however, the generosity of the others had worn thin, and the only ones left to help hide Madame's absence were Minnie and Olympia. Minnie said nothing about it, but doggedly went about the doubled duties as if they were inevitably hers. Between doing her own work and Madame Barbue's as well, however, Olympia was exhausted.

She was so worn, she barely noticed that Diamond took every opportunity to remove herself from Olympia's presence. Once, in the big tent where they took their meals, Olympia almost sat next to Diamond at the large table. Olympia was more than happy to sit there, in the only seat left available, since it seemed like ages since she'd talked to Diamond, but the very moment she slid into her chair, Diamond said a cheerful good night to the entire table and took her plate to the soapy basin where Minnie was doing the washing-up.

"WHERE IS MADAME BARBUE? SHE hasn't performed in days!"

Magnus came storming into the gathering tent. Everyone's head swiveled to see him; all conversation stopped. Olympia was just coming back from taking a meal to Madame Barbue (she left the food on the trailer steps; Barbue would only come out to get it after Olympia had gone if she got it at all; she neglected many meals entirely) and froze as soon as she heard Magnus's voice. He didn't make an appearance among the circus performers and crew very often, and never in the tent where they gathered for meals. He preferred to take his meals alone in his office, to keep himself, as he said, above the fray, but most folks were convinced it was because he neither wanted to associate with them nor to *be* associated with them.

"Barbue is ill tonight," Minnie spoke up. "But she's been working her shows, just like the rest of us!"

"I have it on good authority she has *not*," Magnus told the crowd. He stood awkwardly at the head of the long table with his hands shoved deep in his pockets. Everyone knew those hands would stay there; Magnus rarely let his pincers out in plain sight.

"Who is this authority?" Minnie stood, knocking her chair over as she did so, to glare at the rest of the company one by one. "I'm sure whoever this *authority* is, they are either mistaken or untrustworthy."

"Several of the customers have complained to me that her appearance in the sideshow was advertised, yet she was nowhere to be found," he said.

The performers all began to grumble at once, and Minnie attempted to huff indignantly (though she was not very convincing). Sarah, who was known onstage as Dead-Eyed Susan, banged the table with her fist.

"That's absolute bunk," she shouted. "I have performed in every show in which Madame Barbue has performed since I joined the revue!"

This was technically true; it was simply that the reverse was not, for Madame Barbue had certainly *not* performed in every show that Sarah had. Sarah, as Dead-Eyed Susan, offered a variety act and was not, herself, one of the freaks. She was tall, thin, and entirely intact, and she looked like the twin of Sarah Bernhardt, with an unruly ruffle of curly dark hair and an aquiline nose. She was, by most men's estimation, exceptionally beautiful and was made all the more attractive by her confident swagger and her fearlessness with a gun.

Magnus was a smart man and knew when a battle was lost. He was outnumbered, and loyalty was not on his side.

"Tell Madame," he said calmly to the entire crew, "that she had better resume her work in the show *tomorrow*, or she will no longer have a place with this organization, and we will leave her in this mud pit of a town when we move on."

With that, Magnus turned on his very expensive heel and stormed out of the tent, leaving a stunned and unhappy silence in his wake.

* * *

54

MAGNUS WAS THE SON OF a traveling salesman and a washerwoman. His father, Taddeus, sold tinware from door to door. He was a sad man, slightly bent, whose shoes were always worn out—a man for whom Magnus, by all accounts, should not have been able to muster respect. But by his example, Taddeus taught Magnus when to wheedle and when to cajole, when false cheerfulness and confidence was most effective, and when a conspiratorial air would get you farther.

These things were important for Magnus to learn because, as his parents were sure, he would not be able to survive without tricks. He was born a beautiful, black-haired little baby boy, to be sure, but where his hands should have been were angry red, bulbous things with two claw-like pincers apiece in place of fingers—more like lobster claws than human hands. His mother was so horrified by the sight of them that she couldn't bear to hold the infant, even while he nursed, but bent over the baby, whom she laid on her bed and covered with a sheet, during feedings. At all other times, she covered his hands, for she could not stand the sight of them. She swaddled him until he was nearly eighteen months old, just to ensure that the baby wouldn't wave his claws where anyone else could see.

When he grew so big that she could no longer justify keeping him so tightly swaddled, Lucinda let Magnus's legs free, but hid his hands in thick cotton mitts, which she bound to him securely with twine wrapped around his wrists. He'd spent so much of his early life swaddled that, when he was finally freed, he could not easily walk, but lumbered like a tiny monster, mitts held above his head as he jolted from room to room, and crashed as frequently as he managed to toddle upright. This only horrified his mother further, because he moved nothing like a boy should, and she spent as little time with him as she could manage, though Magnus attempted to follow her everywhere.

When Magnus was three years old, Lucinda met a man—a magician called Strike-O—with whom she fell in love and ran away, leaving Magnus and Taddeus with a sinkful of unwashed dishes and a note that simply read *Please care for Magnus.* She'd left in such a hurry that her hairbrush was still on her vanity and all but one of her dresses still swung in the closet. In her absence, Taddeus neglected to tie the mitts to Magnus's hands and, for the first time in his life, he was allowed to touch: his father's face, the rough upholstery on the settee, the ruffling tickle of grass spears, his own teeth and his own eyelids and his own skin. It was overwhelming and wonderful, and he could not stop, until the day when Taddeus was entertaining their next-door neighbors and little Magnus threw his hands into the folds of the woman's silk dress and would not let go, no matter how loudly she screamed. From that day, Taddeus remembered to tie the mitts around Magnus's hands every time there was even a chance that another person would see him.

Taddeus wrote to his sister, who joined them immediately. Ingebrit was stern, and very clean, and looked almost exactly like Taddeus—skin pale and freckle-dotted, eyes arctic-blue, hands long-fingered and wide—except that she wore a dress and kept her white hair piled high on top of her head. She argued vehemently that, for his own good, Magnus should be sent to an orphanage, where they might care for someone with his condition, but Taddeus wouldn't hear of it. He was, he told her, far too soft for that.

As Magnus grew, Taddeus indulged him at every turn, though he still required the boy to wear cotton mitts in public and taught him to hide his claws in his pockets as an extra precaution against horrifying others. He spent a life without touch, which surely slowed his intellect and isolated him and made loving anyone—including his father—difficult; his life, in all ways, was dulled considerably. Though Taddeus had hoped to train him as a salesman, Magnus simply couldn't accomplish that without showing his hands and thus horrifying his customers. The few times Taddeus took Magnus along as his assistant on sales calls were unbridled disasters.

When Magnus was old enough to fend for himself, his father and Ingebrit took him to see the traveling circus. They sat in the big tent and watched the acrobats and clowns, the trained animal acts, and the woman who played a human cannonball. Then his father brought him into the sideshow tent to see the acts there—the World's Smallest King, the Wild Man from Borneo, the World's Fattest Woman and the World's Thinnest Man—while Ingebrit occupied herself elsewhere. Frankly, Magnus couldn't care less where she was; every moment alone with his father was like a secret gift, and he huddled close and watched his face intently, even though that meant he would miss the wonders of the sideshow. His father's face betrayed no emotion, though, as the moments passed, it grew redder and redder.

When the show was over, Ingebrit joined them outside the tent. She was on the arm of an obsequiously smiling man in a striped suit, who introduced himself to Magnus as Mister Johnson, the Proprietor of This Fine Show. He looked at Magnus as if he were supposed to be impressed, though Magnus wasn't sure why.

"Well," his father said, growing redder.

"Let's go to my office," Mister Johnson said. "I should like to see those claws you've got, young sir."

Magnus froze. He was supposed to keep them hidden, and he'd been very careful while they visited the circus to keep his wrapped claws in his pockets. How Mister Johnson had known—and what the consequences of being discovered would be—he wasn't sure, but he couldn't bear his father's disapproving look.

The four of them climbed into Mister Johnson's trailer, in which he'd set up a large oak desk and a velveteen chair. On the desk was an array of papers, all blotted with ink, and a ridiculously large vase of flowers. Mister Johnson sat behind the desk. Taddeus and Ingebrit stood in front of the desk and steered Magnus to stand in front of them.

"Let us look at those claws you've got, Magnus," Mister Johnson said cheerfully.

Magnus looked, unsure, at his father—this was against every rule he'd ever been taught—but Taddeus simply nodded and reached for Magnus. "Hold up your hands, now," he said and, when Magnus did, he pulled off the mitts with a modest flourish. All three adults—Taddeus, Ingebrit, and Mister Johnson—sighed together.

"Show him," his father said.

Though his instinct was to hide his arms behind his back, at his father's urging, Magnus held his claws out above Mister Johnson's desk.

"Do they move?" Mister Johnson asked his father.

"Yes, of course," Taddeus said. "Open and close!"

Magnus did, stretching his pincers as best he could.

"Extraordinary!" Mister Johnson exclaimed. "May I touch them?" Again, he addressed Taddeus.

"Of course." Taddeus pushed Magnus's arms farther across the desk. Mister Johnson reached out a quivering hand and stroked the top of one of Magnus's claws.

"Extraordinary!" he said again. "I will take it!"

He handed an envelope to Taddeus, saying, "It's what we agreed upon," and nodded profusely. To Magnus he said, "Would you like to meet some of the performers?"

Magnus, of course, would very much have liked that, but he looked to his father to be sure. Taddeus was, if possible, even redder. "You may, Magnus." He softly patted the back of his neck.

"I will take him to the tent," Mister Johnson said. "You two are free to go. We can handle things from here."

"Yes," Taddeus patted the back of Magnus's neck once more. "Be a well-behaved boy, Magnus."

"Thank you," Ingebrit said to Mister Johnson. She put her arm through Taddeus's and together the two left the trailer.

"Let's go meet the Madams Danner and McAvoy," Mister Johnson said, holding out his hand, "and Mister Charles." Magnus paused, looking at the mitts on the desk. "Oh, never mind about those," Mister Johnson said. "You won't need those anymore."

*　*　*

IT WAS NOT UNTIL MAGNUS was almost twenty-two that he met Cora, who came to the circus to work as a clown. She arrived with only a single trunk and kept to herself, only occasionally sharing a meal with the other clowns—and never with anyone else—preferring to spend most of her time wandering alone through the woods beside which the circus always seemed to park its wagons and pitch its tents.

She wore, as a clown, layers upon layers of frilled skirts and petticoats, so that she appeared to be nearly round, and a bright orange wig with two long braids in which she was always tangling herself. He had never once heard her speak, but her pantomime was bright and cheerful and exaggerated in such a way that Magnus knew, upon watching the first time, that he loved her.

Though he had never spoken to her before, he approached her one evening at dinner, asked to sit next to her—to which she politely acquiesced—and spent the evening so nervous that he kept his own hands shoved deep under a napkin on his lap and did not eat at thing.

Cora sat with the group of clowns, the only woman among them, and they jostled each other and drank and told the dirtiest stories they could conjure. They could not, no matter how hard they tried, make her blush—she was rowdy as the best of them, but kind as well. When the other men began to push and tease Magnus, she looked at them sternly, shook her head, and asked what it was exactly that kept Magnus with the circus.

"He's The Human Crustacean!" one of the clowns yelled joyfully.

Magnus shook his head silently, but the clowns were at it now.

"Half human, half undersea creature," another yelled, imitating the barker. "He may have a face like an angel, but his body longs to scuttle the ocean floor!"

"Don't get too close," another laughed, "or he'll nip you to pieces!" At that, the napkin was ripped from Magnus's lap, and his lobster claws were exposed.

Cora did not even look. "Stop it, you cruel beasts!" she cried. "*You are the creatures here!*" With that, she rose, took Magnus by the arm, and pulled him along behind her until they were outside.

"I am sorry for that," Cora whispered. Huge tears had welled up in her eyes and her face was all kindness.

"It's no bother."

"You're being brave," she said. "Come walk with me." She set off toward the woods, and Magnus followed her across the field and into the fringe of trees. The forest floor was spongy with fallen pine needles, and Cora immediately took off her shoes and looped the straps around the ribbon at her waist. They walked in the quiet black of the woods, until Cora stopped and looked Magnus in his eye. "I'm not afraid of you," she said. "You are a kind boy, and those men in there are the true brutes."

"Thank you." Magnus began to warm with hope.

"Let me see them," she told him, and it was clear from the way she cast her eyes to his pockets that she wanted to see his claws.

"Madam—" he began to protest, but she would hear none of it.

"Come now, let me see them. You show all the world that comes to the circus; you may as well show me."

Nervously, Magnus drew his arms upward until his claws hung in the air between them, red and bulbous as ever.

"My," she whispered. Her hands automatically came up to touch, but she stopped herself and asked, "May I touch them?"

"Yes," Magnus whispered. It was the gentlest moment of his life. Cora brought both hands to rest atop his and ran her fingers lightly over the swollen flesh. She looked at him plaintively as she did so, and Magnus felt as if he might die from the sweetness. He wanted so badly to hold her hand, to reach up and touch her face, to return the caress in some way, but he chose to stay still as she touched in wonder. He did not want to break the spell that held them together—and apart from the rest of the world. He submitted to her gaze and her touch.

"How do you hold a pen?" she asked. "How do you button your own trousers?"

"I am able to do most things you can do," Magnus blushed. A little sting began in the pit of his stomach.

"But how?" Cora asked again. "I should like to see you write a letter or comb your hair. I would pay to see it."

"I will show you without pay," Magnus said, as his stomach seemed to melt away, leaving an empty, sinking pit.

"But I would pay to see it!" she cried.

Magnus took the biggest chance of his life then, pulled his claws from her hands, and held her face. He was going to kiss her.

"No, Magnus," she stammered. "No, this is not at all—"

"Once," he pleaded, but it was too late. The heat of her was gone, and the smell of lilacs gone, too, as she turned and ran out of the woods alone.

Magnus did not follow her, but stood by himself in the lightless clearing for a long time. By the time he had dragged himself out of the woods and back to his trailer, she had already fled to her own. She must have left the circus in the middle of that night, because he never saw Cora again.

* * *

MAGNUS REFUSED, FROM THEN ON, to step onstage. He refused to make a show of eating, or buttoning his overcoat, or combing his hair. The set that had been made just for him, which was meant to look like a bachelor's quarters in anyone's town (the overstuffed chair, the vanity, and the wooden closet), languished empty and gathered dust.

Instead, Magnus began to steal. Though he wasn't a successful pickpocket, he was often able to muster convincing enough bluster (when he wore his best suit) to fool simpler folk into giving him money for investments that would, because he never made them, eventually fail. By the time this or that foolish farmer realized that Magnus had stolen his hard-won pennies, Magnus was long gone, busy conning a new poor farmer or struggling shopkeeper or, on one lucky occasion, a rather stupid, newly minted heir.

During all of his work, he kept his hands carefully hidden under silk handkerchiefs and in the pockets of his beautifully cut trousers. He affected such an air of confidence and intelligence that never once did a mark suspect him of empty promises, and often they defended him to the teeth even after he'd robbed them and left town.

Each day, Magnus forgot a little bit more: First to go were the faces of Lucinda and Taddeus and Ingebrit, and then he lost the memory of their scent and their shape, and finally even the memory of their betrayal, until at last he did not remember they'd existed at all. He forgot Mister Johnson entirely. He forgot dinners with the crew, and how it felt to sleep soundly in his trailer while the wagons popped and swayed toward the next town. He forgot how it felt to wake in a new place, and how his arms would burn from hefting the canvas and ropes and pressboard trunks in and out of the wagons. He grew rich enough to replace his two dead teeth with gold ones, so that his smile glinted ominously, metallic, luxe, and unreal, on the rare occasions he gave one.

After less than a year of forgetting, he had wiped clean almost his entire life and was a new, more successful, smug Magnus. Last of all, he forgot Cora. He forgot her rouged lips and her kind voice, and the way she'd risen to his defense against the nastier members of their crew. He forgot the lilac of her perfume. He forgot her horrified rejection, the way she'd pulled away from him and run, alone, back through the woods and was never seen again.

Deliberately, with great effort, he forgot and forgot her, until the day when he forgot her name and, soon after, forgot that she had ever existed.

* * *

WHEN MADAME BARBUE FINALLY EMERGED from her trailer, shaky as a new colt, she did so—after much pleading and cajoling—on Olympia's arm. Olympia escorted her to dinner, where they were greeted by surprised and fond calls and embraces. Madame was given a seat at the head of the table, and Olympia sat at her left side, where she served her and doted on her as much as she was permitted. Absence, in all its forms, frightened Olympia as much as stillness, and Barbue was limp and wordless and still beside her. She acquiesced to every offered helping of food or water but, though she usually had a ravenous appetite at meals, on this night she touched none of what was given her. She allowed others to pilfer food from her plate without protest and, though she was usually the loudest and foulest mouth at the dinner table, on this night she did not speak a word. Olympia worried and fussed over her, which usually would have sent Madame Barbue into a fury. Even a nasty slap and scolding would have been preferable to Barbue's silence. Everyone did their best to distract her with silly conversation and gossip, but she simply sat and stared into space, appearing not even to listen.

After dinner, Ramus escorted her around the grounds, holding her hand against his forearm protectively and speaking low. She nodded seriously at his words, though she contributed little to the conversation herself. Once, however, Minnie, who had been carefully watching them walk, saw her smile and heard her tinkling laugh. When she told Olympia, the two held hands tightly and did not speak about their hope.

Even Diamond, though she still had not spoken to Olympia, endured her presence long enough to visit Madame Barbue. She brought with her a few elaborately frosted napoleons nestled in a pink box sealed with gold foil from a bakery in town. Madame, when she received them, lit to thank her sincerely and then extinguished again, but Diamond was heartened by the glimpse of the old Barbue and stayed for several hours, drinking from the flask Barbue hid in her cupboard and telling the bawdiest of the jokes she'd collected at the dinner table.

The next day, Madame Barbue was back onstage and, though it was not her usual plucky performance and she did it without enthusiasm, she still dressed in her freshly laundered yellow dress, dangled her parasol from her wrist, chomped on the cigar butt, and stroked her freshly beribboned beard. Everyone in the crew sighed because, though she was not herself, she was at least present and Magnus would have no reason to get rid of her. For his part, Magnus left her alone, and did not back up his threats to attend her shows and ensure she went onstage.

It was not until days later, when the performers and crew lined up outside his trailer to receive their weekly stipends, that they realized something was amiss. Nobody had seen Magnus in quite a few days— not since he'd threatened to fire Madame Barbue—and his trailer remained stubbornly quiet and locked tight, no matter how hard the crew banged on the door loudly demanding their due.

Once they had convinced Ramus the situation was dire enough to break down Magnus's door, and once Ramus had ripped the door from its hinges and tossed it aside, as many of them as could fit pushed into the little office to find it completely empty. Magnus had left piles of money, apparently mid-count, on the desk; the ashes of a cigarette dusted the desktop, and a pen lay atop dried ink on the blotter. There was otherwise no sign of Magnus.

"He's skipped out!" someone yelled, and the rest of the men began to yell foul-mouthed insults and fury.

"That greedy little son-of-a-whore penguin!"

"He ran off rather than give us our due!"

It was a long while before Ramus calmly pointed out that Magnus had not taken the money with him, but had left it sitting on his desk in plain view for anyone to take. This was a logical flaw in the accusations, but it didn't seem to slow the mob one bit. Men grabbed the stacks of coins and stuffed their pockets, pushing and squealing like pigs, until the desk was empty and not a coin remained.

Five
The Dead-Eyed Lady

Aside from the day she'd gone walking with Ramus, Madame Barbue had not left her trailer again, but sat all day at the window, hunched in a straight-backed wooden chair and stroking her beard. Once she discovered Magnus was gone, she had no reason to perform her show and she quit. The sideshow had dwindled so profoundly that only a handful of performers kept up their acts anymore. The rest, in the wake of Magnus's departure, feared that they would no longer earn a living and fled in the dead of night, having ransacked their trailers for those goods that could be carried in a suitcase. Every morning, it seemed, another trailer door was left swinging open and another trailer abandoned.

But of all the unforeseen absences the circus now endured, that of Madame Barbue was, perhaps, the most painful, because she was still present in body, but the loving, resolutely cheerful, persistent, hard-edged Madame Barbue appeared to be gone for good.

* * *

The circus drifted. Nobody had understood quite how much Magnus had done to keep them together and to keep, as they said, the show on the road, until he was gone. The pay upon which they all depended dwindled and became an unreliable resource. Food for the company dinner, which, for many of them, was the only meal of the day, became scant, as nobody was sure how much money to allocate to its purchase, and, without Magnus's whip-crack discipline hanging over them, few helped prepare meals, wash dishes, or procure goods for the cooks anymore. How long they should linger in any one town was a point of heated contention; where to park the caravan of trailers and pitch the tents became a nearly unsolvable dilemma, since Magnus's town-to-town contacts seemed to have disappeared along with him.

Diamond valiantly struggled to keep up her act, even though she was not being regularly paid or fed (and the shelter of the tents and trailers was rapidly falling to tatters). She became, in the absence of Barbue and the vanished performers, an important fixture of the sideshow.

One afternoon, when the audience was unusually large and rowdy and Diamond's performance was buoyed by gasps of horror and delight, the hammer dropped. Just as Diamond carefully slid a sword down her throat, just as Minnie on the accordion held a long and dramatic note to heighten the experience, and just as the crowd held its breath—at the moment when all these things happened, a woman in the back of the crowd screamed.

The crowd was a good one, eager and gamely packed into the sweaty, mildewing tent. One of the crew, Dolor, who sometimes worked as a clown and sometimes as a rigger, was squeezing his stealthy way through the pressed bodies, feeling pockets and purses for change to steal. (Now that Magnus was gone, several of the crew, unbridled, had taken to grift.) At precisely the instant that Diamond had slipped the long, thin sword down her throat and was holding her pose so that the crowd could be put properly in awe, Dolor slipped his hand around the waist of a woman in the back row in order to fumble into the pocket of the man next to her. The woman, feeling Dolor's hand at her waist, screamed.

"Help! Get your paws off, you creep!"

The crowd erupted into a brawl as several men jumped on Dolor and began beating him, and, soon after, more men jumped into the fray. Fists missed their mark and inevitably hit innocent people, who then furiously clocked whomever was closest, and, within moments, a wholesale brawl had broken out, into which even the most proper ladies in the audience were drawn.

Diamond, hearing shrieks, began carefully to withdraw the sword—just in case—but did not do it quickly enough. As the energy of the fight mounted, a young man was hurled out of the fray and came rolling onto the stage, knocking into Diamond's leg and sending the sword sideways in her gullet. Once she had pulled the sword entirely free of her mouth, she spat several mouthfuls of blood and then fainted in a limp heap.

Screams and whistles did nothing to still the fighting, and some of the crewmen threw themselves into it and began yanking up the most enthusiastic of the participants and carrying them to the end of the midway, where they were unceremoniously tossed out. Still, it took almost half an hour to clear out enough of the violent ones that the crowd could—warily—mill about, grumbling, edging its way to the exits. Onstage, Diamond remained crumpled on the floor, her sword clattered somewhere beneath the seats. Ramus knelt at her side and held her bloody mouth open to help her breathe. Blood soaked the front of her costume, soaked the floorboards beneath her, and coated Ramus's hands in just a few moments.

As deftly as he could, Ramus picked up her body and carried her to her trailer, where he laid her on her side in the bed. One of the clowns had been sent running for the doctor as soon as Diamond fell, but Ramus was afraid he would return too late.

A DOCTOR HAD COME WITHOUT much sense of urgency, looked at Diamond a bit disdainfully, and suggested that she needed simply to rest as she was and that she should be carefully watched and attended to, but that she was to eat no food for the next several days, drink no water for at least a day, and avoid shoving dangerous objects down her throat, well, always.

Just as the doctor left, there was a furious banging on the door, enough almost to knock it off its hinges. Ramus opened the door to find Madame Barbue, haphazardly dressed, with a kerchief over her hair, but awake and sharp-eyed.

"Is she dead?" Madame Barbue asked him, pressing into the trailer without excusing herself. Ramus didn't care.

"She's not dead," Ramus said. "The doctor was just here. He said she needs to rest and she cannot have food or drink for a while. She's still asleep, though."

Madame Barbue barely heard Ramus. She stood at the foot of the cot, looking at Diamond, who lay on her side with her arms and legs dropping off the edge of the bed as if she'd been hurled there carelessly. She was white as the flesh of an apple; her lips were starkly red with dried blood.

"She's so pale," Barbue moaned and dropped to her knees next to the bed. Ramus pulled up a chair and lifted Madame Barbue to sit in it, and she stayed there—would stay there, unwavering in her focus, for the entire day. Ramus squatted on the floor next to Barbue and put his hand on her arm.

"The doctor never said she wouldn't recover," he reasoned. "In point of fact, he specifically told us not to give her food for a few days, which means he imagined she might open her eyes and ask for some."

Madame neither looked at him nor spoke. She only shook her head, never taking her eyes from Diamond's face.

"She's a tough girl and she knows we're all waiting on her," he tried. "She'll come back."

Ramus attempted, on several occasions, to get Madame Barbue to eat or drink something, but she was wild and angry, and would not look away from Diamond, as though Barbue knew that the moment she ceased to look at her, Diamond would slip away into death. Despite Madame's vigilance, Diamond stayed pale and still; the parting of her bloody lips on a wheeze of air was the only indication that she was still alive.

* * *

OLYMPIA COULD DO NOTHING. SHE could not practice, nor could she wash dishes, because the tent reminded her of Diamond. She couldn't go for a walk in the nearby wood, since they had walked there together that morning, and she couldn't go anywhere on the grounds without being reminded of the bloody scene of Diamond's accident by some well-meaning person or another—it was the only thing about which anybody wanted to talk. Olympia couldn't even hide in her own trailer, because the absence of Madame Barbue was a palpable void reminding her that Barbue, wracked with terror, was spending all her spare moments at Diamond's bedside. There was nowhere she could go that didn't make her think of Diamond, and so she chose to sit outside Diamond's trailer in the mud, rest her back against the metal siding, and draw letters in the dirt with a stick. That made her remember her father, who taught her to do that very thing when she was young and still learning to write.

From inside the trailer came, occasionally, the muffled wails of Barbue, and every once in a while, someone would pass by, look at Olympia strangely, and keep going, but Olympia continued to sit as resolutely as if it were a vigil. She was not sure which was worse: the immediate blink-out-and-gone of her parents' disappearance or Diamond's slow slip out of the world.

* * *

SARAH, THE SHARPSHOOTER WHO WAS called Dead-Eyed Susan onstage, was newest to the traveling show and so, though fraught with grief and fear for Diamond, she stayed a respectful distance away from the trailer while she ailed and her friends mourned. When Diamond fell, Sarah had been there, and had dropped to her knees alongside Ramus in the blood on the stage floor. She still had the dress she'd been wearing—her costume, a buckskin coat and a fringed brown sheath underneath—but it was soaked to the waist with blood and she despaired of ever getting it clean enough to wear onstage again. It was a small matter, about which she cared little, but the dress, which she had hung on a hook on the wall of her trailer, was a constant reminder of the awful scene she'd been helpless to fix.

Sarah understood blood, in a way even the toughest farm wife did not. Her family had lived in a one-room cabin at a lake's edge in Tennessee. She'd had one older brother and four younger, all of whom had been skilled hunters who taught her to hunt as soon as she was able to lift the heavy shotgun. Her brother David had barely lived to five years old when, running in the woods, he was accidentally taken for a deer and shot to death. Ket and Sarah had carried his body home in a mess of smeared blood and tears.

Sarah had practiced shooting cloth targets until she earned the nickname Dead-Eyed Susan—like the flower, Ket told her, but much more dangerous—and she proudly imagined herself an outlaw. She was only thirteen years old when her mother became pregnant again, and Sarah, understanding all too clearly how limited their resources were and how little she was able to contribute to the home, left.

She traveled north to Michigan and found work in a paper mill. She lived in the wood dormitory and spent long days on the mill line, counting out and weighing reams of newly bleached, newly trimmed paper, which was sometimes still a bit wet from the processing line. Her hands turned white and wrinkled and were slashed with tiny red cuts from handling the paper. They were so ugly and sore that Sarah wore a pair of white cotton gloves nearly everywhere she went.

One Sunday, Sarah ventured into town with a small group of the other women who worked on the mill line and met a man who wanted to take her away.

Sarah and her friends had sought lunch in the dining room of an inn, where they were disturbed through their entire meal by a posse of foul-mannered young men drinking at a nearby table. The men were already thoroughly pickled and, apparently, starved for affection of any sort. Sarah's friends cowered and ate their soup as quickly as they could, eager to leave and get away from the crass boys who were, at that very moment, whispering lewd remarks in their direction.

"I'll have that miss there," said one of the boys. He leered at Colette, traced an hourglass shape in the air, and whistled. He was a sicklier green than the rest of them and was tall and thin and gap-toothed when he smiled.

"She's got a sweet face," said another, "but I'll have that one in the corner, who looks scared as a lamb. You're not frightened of me, are you, my little lamb?"

The girl in question shook a bit, and Sarah clenched her fists.

"Enough! Stop this!" She whirled on the men, who looked momentarily surprised before recovering their leers.

"Aw, darling, I'll take you any day," said one of the boys, slapping his thigh. "I like the big, feisty ones. You just need a good spanking."

Without thought, Sarah hiked up her skirt and drew the little pistol from where she'd strapped it against the side of her knee. She pointed the gun directly at the last boy's head, then deliberately moved her hand ever so slightly to the left and fired. The bullet whizzed past his face, just barely missing his cheek, and lodged in the far wall.

"Blasted cow!" he shrieked, holding his cheek and dropping to the ground. "She nearly shot me!"

"You're lucky she aims as poorly as she behaves," one of his friends said.

"Or perhaps she aims very well and fancies you for herself," said another man, whose words were met with raucous laughter.

"Shut your dirty mouths," Sarah said, still aiming the gun at the group of boys. "And leave us proper folk to our meal."

"Sweetheart, if you come and sit with us, we'll buy you your meal," the first man said in a syrupy voice.

"And there's no need to be proper, either," another one said, and the whole bunch of them snickered and whistled.

Sarah raised the gun again, and one of the girls who sat with her whispered, "Sarah, put that away, they're just having a bit of fun." Sarah shook her off and refocused her aim on one of the more raucous, red-faced fellows.

"That's quite enough of that," said the bartender. "You ladies should leave now, I think. Go back to the paper mill."

Spoons and china clattered as the women stood, practically as one, and hustled to leave the inn. Colette wound her arm around Sarah's waist.

"Come with us, Sarah, and leave these boys here to rot in their own filth," she said loudly, pulling her toward the door. Once they were all out on the street, the crowd of women seemed to grow braver, and lingered there, in no hurry to leave.

But not a moment later they scattered, shrieking, when the tavern door burst open and a man—red-haired, mustachioed, fairly lit, and flushed bright as a boiled sugar beet—tumbled out as if he had been tossed.

"Misses," he said, bowing low and tipping his hat for the women. "I apologize for those brutes in there. They behave as if they've never been in the presence of a lady, as if their mothers and sisters were not women."

Some of the girls tittered behind their hands, but stepped away and huddled together, glancing warily at the man, who was attempting to dust himself off and wipe an inordinate amount of sweat off his neck. When he stood upright again, he walked straight to Sarah and bowed.

"Miss, I hope you will forgive me for asking, but I was utterly astonished at your bravery and skill with those boys in there," he said. "Or, rather, with that pistol of yours. Those boys just got in the way. You *were* intending to miss that boy, yes?"

Sarah laughed. "Yes, sir. I didn't want to draw blood, only to draw off the hounds."

"Can you do it again? Can you, say, hit the top of that fence post from here?" He pointed to a nearby fence post, but Sarah shook her head.

"I shall hit the next one farther," she scoffed. "The one you chose is too simple."

The man laughed and held up a hand to tell her to wait, then ran to the fence post in question and balanced atop it a rock. "Can you make that?"

"Easily," Sarah said and, with barely a look, raised her pistol and shot the rock, sending it flying upward. Some of the girls screamed, but the man simply shook his head and let out a low whistle.

"You are a mighty good shot." He bowed again. "Can you do it a second time?"

"Of course, sir, but let us make it the next post, just for fun." She pointed down the line. The next post was only four feet farther away, but it probably seemed impressive to up the ante.

The man grinned, ran to the post, and placed another rock atop it. He turned and ran back to stand behind Sarah and said, "If you make this one, I can guarantee you a job, and it won't break your back, either."

"Thank you, sir." Sarah aimed, then tipped her head back dramatically to look at the sky, and shot. The rock skittered off the post, as she'd known it would.

He bowed even lower, and Sarah laughed again at his attempts at courtliness when he was as dirty and shaggy as a homeless badger. "I would like to offer you work. I think there is a place for you with my outfit," he said.

Sarah tied the gun back at the side of her knee, discreetly reaching under her skirt to do so, then looked at him as she straightened. "Sarah!" a couple of the girls cowering behind her whispered. Sarah clasped her hands together; they stung, as always, from the papermaking chemicals and the thousand tiny cuts they bore. She hated the paper mill, and she smelled on this man the possibility of escape. "Which outfit is that?" she asked.

"The Stephens Great Attraction," he said. "We are a traveling show. I would like to bring you with us. I think you could have something like a Wild Prairie Shooting Show."

"I see," she said.

"Sarah, no," one of the girls whispered to her. "It's a circus." The other girls, cowed, refused even to speak in this man's presence.

"It is, indeed, miss." He bowed to the lady who'd whispered a bit more loudly than she'd intended. He turned to Sarah. "It's true that we have a traveling show, but the pay is steady, your act would be very popular, you'd get to see the country, and we have many respectable women working with us. We live like a family."

"I see," said Sarah again, but in her mind she was already packing her bag. The word "family" had great effect, for she missed her own immensely.

The man bowed yet again and then held out his arm for her to take. "May I take you to the Attraction to meet everyone, so that you might decide with more information?"

Sarah took his arm, although behind her she could hear the scandalized whispers of the other girls from the paper mill. "But you can't!" "What will your parents say?" "You don't even know this man!"

"Please, miss, forgive me for not introducing myself properly," the man said, eyeing the girl who'd whispered the last protest. "I am Ramus and I am the Strongest Man Alive."

"Then I'm sure you'll make an excellent escort." Sarah steeled herself and looped her arm through his.

* * *

SARAH AGREED, WITHOUT A MOMENT'S hesitation, to become Dead-Eyed Susan. Once Ramus had escorted her to the circus grounds and taken her to meet the rest of the troupe, she was wholly convinced she'd found her place. As odd a collection of folk as they were—and they seemed to represent the absolute limits of humanity, very tall or very short, exceptionally skilled or oddly formed—they were welcoming and kind and seemed to Sarah absolutely familiar. Even the man in charge, Mister Stephens, was cordial and interested to see her skills with a gun, and, once he witnessed a demonstration, immediately offered her lodging and pay and the safety of their small traveling family.

Along with Madame Barbue, Minnie, Ramus, and two men whom Sarah assumed, since they were not introduced, were simply present for their muscle, Sarah went to her dormitory at the paper mill, and, between the six of them, they loaded all her possessions into a cart in a matter of minutes. After leaving her notice and giving a few of the girls tearful embraces and promises of letters to come, Sarah left the paper mill far behind and for good, carried off in the back of a wagon and intent on joining the circus.

* * *

SARAH DRESSED IN A FRINGED buckskin sheath. She put her hair in two long braids and rouged her lips and cheeks as red as she could and became, quite suddenly, Dead-Eyed Susan. Though her dress was short and her face was painted, the part of her costume that caused the greatest scandal was her shoes: She wore none.

She shot targets and built from tricks with a bow and arrow (which she shot at spinning targets, sometimes, or human targets whom she would deliberately and narrowly miss) to tricks with her pistol and from simple shots to blindfolded shots to shots she took over her shoulder while facing the opposite direction. She never missed, and the crowd was always wild for her. She represented a perfect combination of danger and beauty, and each afternoon she performed, at least one man hollered out a marriage proposal. Every time, Sarah laughed, shrugged and, in lieu of an answer, shot—without looking—another impressively difficult target.

During her final show—though nobody, least of all Sarah, suspected it was such—Sarah performed with such a rare combination of accuracy and flair that she could not stop her own enthusiasm. The longer she performed, the more confident she grew, dramatically turning her back and flinging her arm to cover her eyes as she took the final shots. The crowd was, at even its quietest moments, roaring for her. She crossed her arm over her shoulder and shot as if it had only just occurred to her to do so, as if she didn't care where the bullet went, and, without fail, it hit its mark dead center. It was a night on which Sarah could do absolutely nothing wrong.

The climax of her act was to toss into the air a silk bag filled with a small amount of gunpowder, so that when she shot it, it created a minor—but loud and impressive—explosion midair. At the sound, Sarah threw her gun up and pinned it to the far wall with a perfectly aimed arrow. (By this time the gun was no longer loaded, in case she missed her shot and it crashed to the ground and fired. The intention was to *look* dangerous without actually *being* so.) But on this day, when it seemed nothing could go wrong, something went terribly, terribly wrong.

Sarah pitched the bag of gunpowder high above her head and fired. The resulting explosion was loud, as she'd come to expect, but it produced, unexpectedly, a thick, black cloud of smoke which enveloped the stage, the audience, and Sarah herself. Shouts rang out among the crew and the audience, all of whom waved frantically to send the smoke out of the open tent flap.

When the air had cleared, Sarah was gone. Her gun was spinning on the ground where she'd stood, but no other trace of her remained. One of the crewmen, Thomas, bent to pick up the gun and jumped back, whimpering and holding his red and blistering hand above his head. The gun was hot as lit coals. It remained so for days.

* * *

OLYMPIA STAYED BY DIAMOND'S BED day and night, slept bent over in a chair with her head resting on her knees, and jumped at every slight sound. She spoke to Diamond quietly and wiped her forehead with a wet rag. The blood had been mopped from her lips and her bloody dress removed, so that there was no trace of color on her, and she looked frighteningly waxen. Every once in a while, Olympia tapped Diamond's cheeks and called her name, hoping she would answer, but Diamond continued to sleep.

When she finally woke, it seemed to happen out of nowhere, in the middle of the night. Olympia had fallen asleep on a pillow of her own arms, leaning on the foot of Diamond's cot.

"I had an awful dream," Diamond said into the dark.

Olympia sat bolt upright, sure she'd dreamed the voice until she looked and found Diamond sitting upright, her eyes glittering in the dark, looking right at Olympia.

"You've come back!" she shouted and lunged to throw her arms around Diamond's neck. Diamond winced.

"Easy," she croaked. "That's terrible."

Olympia seemed to remember herself and let go. She sat back and smoothed Diamond's hair over her shoulders.

"I'm sorry," she said. "It's just that you've been sleeping for days, and I wasn't sure you'd wake up again."

Diamond looked at her strangely and smiled. "Of course I'm awake. It was just a bit of a slip."

"You remember it?"

"Why wouldn't I remember?" she asked. "That woman screamed, and my sword slipped, and I gutted myself like a fish." She looked at her belly, felt around for bandages, and then smiled. "Though it appears things weren't that bad; I've not even been patched up."

"You were nearly dead for days," Olympia told her seriously. "You bled everywhere. It was a horrible scene, and you fainted, and they couldn't revive you."

"I seem to have come through it okay," Diamond said. "Though everything hurts something awful."

"I imagine it does. There was so much blood."

Within moments, there was banging on the trailer door and, when Olympia answered, Madame Barbue pushed her way inside, followed closely by Ramus and Minnie.

"Ramus heard voices," Madame Barbue said breathlessly.

"Is she awake?" Minnie asked.

"She most certainly is," Diamond coughed. "And she's sore and unhappy."

"Child! Don't you *ever* give me a fright like this again!" Madame Barbue rushed to her bedside and cupped Diamond's face in her hands, kissing every inch of her cheeks. Minnie and Ramus hung back in the doorway, sheepishly waiting.

"Please come in!" Diamond called in a raspy voice. "Pull this devil of a woman off me! Her love tends to be painful!"

Minnie and Ramus rushed in and pulled Madame Barbue into a chair, though it was clear to everyone there that Diamond wasn't at all bothered by her caresses, painful as they might be.

"You must forgive Madame Barbue's enthusiasm. It's just that we thought you were done for," Ramus said, and Madame Barbue sent him the most awful, glowering look she could muster.

"Olympia has just been telling me this." Diamond patted Olympia's hip.

The rest of the evening passed in quiet celebration. Madame Barbue and Minnie told Diamond about everything that had happened since her injury, including the disappearance of Sarah.

"Dead-Eyed Susan?" Diamond asked.

"Gone without a trace, just like the others," Madame Barbue nodded. "Now there's hardly any of us left."

"Enough of this," Minnie said kindly. "Diamond must be exhausted, and this talk won't help. We are fine as a circus, and everyone is fine enough who's here, now that you're recovered." She patted Diamond's arm. "We will leave you to sleep," she said pointedly, glaring at Madame Barbue.

"Yes," said Barbue. "It's late. Minnie's going to sleep in my trailer tonight, and Olympia will stay here with you." She closed her eyes and placed a lingering kiss on Diamond's forehead, as if Diamond were a little girl having trouble falling asleep. "I am so glad to have you back," she whispered and left before she burst into tears.

"Good night." Ramus held his hand to Diamond's cheek before following Madame Barbue.

"We will be nearby," Minnie said. "If you need us, please send Olympia to fetch us, and we'll come immediately. But I expect you're more likely to sleep than to need us tonight." She paused, then said softly, "I'm glad you're back safely with us." With that, she left, closing the trailer door gently behind her.

OLYMPIA BARELY SLEPT THAT NIGHT.

Though Diamond slept fairly soundly, Olympia worried for most of the night, and would not lie down in the other bed. She slumped in the chair next to Diamond's cot, laid her head near Diamond's hip, and listened to the soft rattle of her breath. Her body ached and she felt dizzy with exhaustion, but she refused to move even the five feet away to the other cot. She kept one hand on Diamond's stomach so she could, all night, feel the soft rise and fall of her belly as she breathed.

In the morning, when Olympia woke (stiff, aching, and ravenously hungry), Diamond was already awake and staring quietly out the window.

"Diamond?" Olympia asked.

"I was just thirsty," Diamond said, "and hungry and trying not to think about it."

Outside, Olympia could hear the distant noises of the riggers striking the tents for the move to the next town—whistles and shouts, the ruffle of canvas, and the slam of metal against wood. She drew in a long breath and took Diamond's hand in her own.

"I love you," she whispered.

"I know," Diamond said, looking terrified.

"What I mean is that I'm so glad you're alive and well. I missed you. And," she added, "I'm sorry for what happened in town."

"It was not so awful at all," Diamond smiled. "You rescued me."

This was not what Olympia had meant, and she was fairly certain that Diamond knew it but was offering a bit of forgetfulness to help them erase her attempted kiss from their history. She took it, gratefully.

Diamond slept on and off all day. Olympia didn't leave her side even to help with striking the tents and packing the caravan for the trip to the next town. Instead, she fetched a pot of water so that it would be ready for Diamond to drink when she was able, and fussed with the curtains on her trailer until exactly the right amount of daylight was allowed to filter in, and smoothed the bedclothes around Diamond's waist and ribs.

"Stop fussing," Diamond mumbled, slowly waking. "You're as bad as Barbue."

"She's a wonderful mother to us all," Olympia said defensively.

"She's kind, but I don't need a mother. I have my own family."

Olympia looked at her strangely, then cleared her throat and looked away.

"You don't believe me?" Diamond asked.

"You're alone here. You came alone, and I have never once seen you send a letter to anyone."

Diamond turned her head away, so that she stared out the trailer window, and was silent for a very long time, so long that Olympia thought she'd fallen asleep again.

"I'm not alone here." She looked pointedly at Olympia. "I have you, and Barbue, and Minnie, and Ramus, and a whole town's worth of people in this show."

"Have you no family of your own, no mother or father, no uncles or sisters out there somewhere looking for you?"

"Haven't *you*?" Diamond asked her testily.

"I thought you'd heard the story," Olympia said. "My parents were the first ones to disappear."

Diamond reddened and was silent for a long time. Finally, she inhaled deeply—which made her wince—and said, "I'm sorry. I had no idea."

"Oh. I thought everyone knew."

Diamond shook her head and mouthed, "Not me," then visibly steeled herself to say, "I had a husband and a baby not yet a year old, and I left them behind in Volusia."

"Oh," Olympia said, because she could not think of anything else to say. "It's fine. What's past is past."

"No," sighed Diamond. "He was an awful man, but Dahlia was a sweet baby. I miss her and I still dream about her every night. By now, she'll be walking."

There was nothing Olympia could say in response; if she argued, it would be out of inexperience, and if she offered platitudes, they would sound false and—worse yet—flimsy. She reached for Diamond's hand atop the sheet and held it tightly.

"What's past will never be past and it will never go away," Diamond said and looked pointedly at Olympia. "What did Shakespeare say? 'What's past is prologue.' I will always have left them." She paused for a very long time, considering, before she put her hand on Olympia's cheek. "And you will always have kissed me, and I will always have pulled away. And I will always have kissed you and you will always have let me."

With that, she drew Olympia's face down to hers and pressed her lips against Olympia's mouth in a lingering, tearful kiss. Olympia did as Diamond had predicted and let her.

Six
The Sprites of the Air

RUMORS OF THE CIRCUS'S TROUBLES—RIOTS in the audience, a missing owner, a dwindling cast of performers—spread faster than the circus itself could travel, and by the time they'd moved into a new town, people were already afraid to go to the show. Only the most daring, the most rowdy, drunk, or desperate would attend. This made for a paltry audience, though the few it comprised were riled up and ready for trouble before they took their seats.

Still, they pressed on to each new town, set up the tents, and put on the show, albeit with as much extra muscle as they could to staff the tent doors. It was mostly for show, mostly to keep the drunks quiet and orderly; Ramus and the crew, who stood with arms folded and stern faces near the exits, never once had to do more than give a lady directions to the grounds entrance.

When the show reached the Georgia border, the wagons suddenly stopped, and it wasn't until Barbue and Ramus investigated that they found the driver's seat of every wagon in the caravan empty all at once. Nobody who remained could figure what happened, since every last horse was still hitched, stomping and irritated by the stillness and the heat of their leathers, with their reins hanging slack on the saddle knobs. Barbue and Ramus ran from wagon to wagon, pounded on the trailer doors and checked to ensure that everyone else was all right, and discovered that every last crewman and rigger was, inexplicably, gone, along with the drivers.

Minnie and Barbue did their best to stem the panic among the remaining performers and to recruit those skilled enough to drive the wagons the remaining few miles to the next town. They arrived a bit later than planned, but miraculously unharmed despite the amateur drivers, and began to unload the wagons. The canvas for the tents was rolled out and spread in a good, open field. Barbue, barking supervisory orders at the lot of them, realized that few of the remaining performers understood how to rig the tents and equipment. They devised a system in which those few in the know supervised a crew of unskilled hands, performers whose strength was needed to hoist the canvas, but who could do nothing more than follow directions. With this system, the entire group—those who remained—hoisted and grunted the show into existence. Each of the performers who knew his or her own equipment best was responsible for rigging it. Within a few hours, the tents and equipment were put up, and the lot of them—dirty, exhausted, and foul-tempered, but victorious—collapsed for the evening without supper because they were too tired to eat.

The first sign of *serious* trouble did not come until the next morning, when the sideshow tent, without so much as a creak or a snap in warning, collapsed and had to be erected again before they began taking tickets from the waiting crowd. Ramus had strained his back while helping to hoist the tents the first time, so he sat to the side, called orders to the crew and felt, in general, fairly helpless and frustrated. Olympia brought him a jar of cool water, but he remained red-faced and het up.

"Pull it tighter or it's going to fall again!" he shouted at the makeshift rigging crew.

"We've got her as tight as she'll go," one of the men yelled.

"No, you don't! It looks just the same as yesterday. If we'd done it right yesterday, we wouldn't be doing it again today!" Ramus shouted.

"Ramus," Olympia scolded gently, "please calm down. If you get any more red and sweaty, you're going to fall over dead."

"If we can't get the tents up without the riggers, *we're* going to fall over dead."

"It's not as if—" Olympia started, then stopped. She was going to say, "It's not as if the fate of all of us rests on your shoulders," but it seemed as though Ramus thought of himself a bit like that other strong man, Atlas, and would vehemently argue with her, so she let the comment go.

Ramus had been taking each disappearance personally. "They're trying to get rid of us," he said to Barbue and the lot of them at breakfast one morning. It didn't matter that no one had any idea why people were disappearing, or whether there was a "They" responsible; Ramus was sure it had something to do with the hostile folks crowding the streets in the towns through which they passed. He had a strong disdain for most outsiders, whom he called "rubes", though it had taken him less than a day to warm up to Diamond. He had accepted her quickly and without question, as soon as she indicated she wanted to join them. The Attraction was Ramus's family, and he was entirely devoted to it; it didn't matter whether he liked them all (he detested most of the clowns), he trusted them against all outsiders and worked hard to keep the family tightly knit and safe from incursions by police and those who meant them ill.

Ramus was, in Olympia's mind, a bit of a stereotype: Scrawny as a kid, he'd spent several long summers trying to put on muscle to avoid the thrice-weekly beatings he suffered at the hands of bullies. It was bad enough that he was parentless, left on the doorstep of a church when he was less than a year old and raised there by the nuns, isolated from other kids and taught day in and day out to recite prayers, count his rosaries, and enumerate his sins in weekly confessions. It was bad enough that his best friend until he was twelve was a nun called Margaret, though what God had failed to bless her with in beauty (she was leather-skinned, wart-faced, and sallow) He had made up for in compassion and intelligence and a great throwing arm. It was bad enough that Ramus tried, daily, to be *good* and thus spent most of his days out of the company of other kids, who were more interested in throwing a good game of craps or trying to frighten women on the street than in reciting prayers or throwing a ball around with a haggard nun. But the fact that Ramus was also small—short and scrawny, sickly and weak—was the straw that broke the camel's back and rang the death knell on his chances of ever finding a true friend.

When he was twelve, he made a program for becoming more muscled. He swallowed as much red meat as he could manage (living with nuns had its disadvantages in this department, for they were poor enough that meat was often hard to come by), and began to lift heavy rocks in an attempt to get stronger. Within a year, he was still squat but considerably thicker and, after several unsuccessful tangles with Ramus, the bullies began to leave him alone. This was exactly the eventuality for which Ramus had hoped, and yet he discovered that without the regular harassment and beatings, he was left nearly without contact with anyone except the nuns. Nobody spoke to him or acknowledged his presence, nor did anyone once throw an arm around his shoulders and invite him into a game. Without the bullies' attention, Ramus had none at all, and he wasn't sure which situation he preferred.

Sister Margaret and the other nuns were wonderful mothers—he had seven of them—and he stayed with them loyally, helping to fix their aging and rapidly crumbling home, until he was nearly twenty. The nuns were quite poor, he noticed, while the priests who lived nearby did not take a vow of poverty and were rewarded with a beautiful home and well-appointed pantry; Ramus thought this extremely unfair, and it only increased his desire to protect and care for the nuns, whom he loved fiercely, and to reject the faith the priests represented, which he discovered he did not love at all. He took any job he could find and brought all the money to the nuns, until he discovered that most of it was summarily dropped into the poor box and *not*, as he'd hoped, used to help feed and care for the nuns themselves.

Even knowing this, Ramus worked harder to bring the nuns more money (though the money was not going to them, he reasoned, it was at least going to something about which they seemed to care deeply) and to keep the home in good repair, until the day Margaret took him aside and told him that he could not stay with them any longer, that he must strike out on his own and find a place to live and something to do with his life. Ramus was never sure whether Margaret was doing him a kindness, trying to push him gently out of the nest and free him from his attachment to the nuns, or whether, as she told him, it really was a problem to have a grown man living with a convent full of brides of Christ.

So, that morning when the tent collapsed and had to be re-erected felt quite familiar to Ramus, as he was used to seeing the walls falling down around the people he loved, and he nearly worked himself—and everyone else—sick to fix it. By the time they were ready to put on the show, the crowd had dwindled; many of them wandered off for a better time at the shops and tavern in town. Little by little, all morning, things failed: Poles listed, ropes snapped, and the spotlight rolled off its stand and shattered when it careened out of the tent and into a trailer wheel. Without the riggers, it seemed, the equipment was staging a protest and refused to function.

Still, the show went on, and the audience that had remained seemed neither to mind nor even to notice when things went wrong. To those who knew the acts well, however, it was a disaster. Samu dropped his whip while disciplining his bear Viselik, and the bear simply stopped roaring and sat, like the sweet oaf he was, and waited until Samu had recovered and could go on. (This was, given the possibilities inherent in an unchained wild bear, perhaps the best outcome for which one might hope, but the absence of the drama of Samu's stern control and Viselik's fierce resistance spoiled the show considerably.) Olympia lost her focus and nearly fell disastrously during her wire walk. General Error tripped upon exiting the clown car and nearly broke his nose; though he recovered himself quickly, those close enough could see tears of pain on his cheeks. The Mistakes of Nature, the troupe of clowns that performed with him, were similarly uncoordinated and sloppy.

The highlight of the main tent show, now that so many performers had disappeared, was the Flying Mirnov Family, World-Famous Russian Aerialists, Sprites of the Air. Olympia could get through no circus show without watching their act, even though it produced quite a bit of pain in her to see another family on the swings when she, herself, was grounded and her family gone. She usually wished the Mirnov Family ill out of spite, hoping one of them would slip and plummet to the net below, unharmed but humiliated enough that the whole lot of them would slink off in the middle of the night and never show their faces in the Attraction again.

When the trapeze cables came loose just as one of the brothers had hurled himself onto it, then, Olympia felt a small pang of guilt for all the ill-wishing she'd done. The trapeze swung violently wrong, tossing the Mirnov into the blackness at the top of the tent, where he seemed to disappear with no more than a small scream. A second cable broke, and a second trapeze tipped sideways, shaking off another Mirnov and hurling her wailing toward the net below. She never arrived, but disappeared somewhere in the unlit distance between the swing and the net.

From then on, it was chaos, as the remaining Mirnovs—like the audience—panicked. Some attempted to escape and went skittering down the ladders, but disappeared along the way and never made it to the ground. Others attempted to press on, flinging themselves tumbling into the dangerous air, only to find no arms to catch them and an empty swing dipping in and out of the spotlight. Mirnov by Mirnov this went on, until there was only one Flying Mirnov left: a young woman who stood quivering on the tiny deck, holding the bar of a swing that had lost its cables. Seeing everyone gone, she leapt and somersaulted in the air, then fell down out of the spotlight toward the net.

By the time the spotlight had caught up to her (one must forgive the poor spotlight that, in the absence of the riggers and crew, was operated by Ramus himself), she was gone.

THE DISASTER ON THE SWINGS ended in absolute pandemonium. The spotlight searched crazy circles on the dark air; the audience stumbled—wild and shocked—out of the tent, bumping and pushing and pressing in their desperation to flee the place. Afterward, like a horrible echo of an earlier day Olympia could not forget, the tent was empty and strangely silent. Instead of helping the searchers—an experience which was likely to be full of too many awful memories of the night her own parents had disappeared—Olympia snuck out without a word to anyone.

She found Diamond waiting for her on the steps of her trailer.

"That was in plain sight," Diamond observed. "That was awful."

"Whatever's happening, at least you're still here," Olympia said.

"Whatever's happening, if it gets much worse, we might all be gone soon."

Diamond brushed her hand along Olympia's arm, and Olympia wanted to grab it and run as far from the tents and the disappearances and disasters as they could get. She couldn't bring herself to say anything in response to Diamond—she knew she was right—so she simply nodded, and the two hurriedly went inside the trailer where it was curtained and quiet.

They kept the lights off, kept the door closed, knowing this time that they needed to be discreet. Whereas earlier moments may have been an innocent unfolding, this time they both knew when they entered the trailer what was going to happen—it was why they entered in the first place. The kissing, however, was bitter.

Diamond pulled away only seconds after they started. "Have the curtains been closed?"

"Yes," Olympia said, "and the door. We're safe. Nobody will see." She tried to bring her mouth back to Diamond's, but Diamond pulled away again.

"Are you sure no one sees us?" she asked, tears glistening under her eyes.

"Nobody sees us," Olympia said. When she was not onstage, she was so easily invisible, even when not technically so, and she was used to the advantage of not being noticed at all. "And if they do see us," she added, just to calm Diamond further, "they're just going to see that we're best friends. You're my greatest friend in the world."

"I want to just *tell* everyone already," Diamond said. "I want everyone to know, no matter what—I just want to stop being careful, to stop thinking all the time. It's exhausting."

"If we tell, if anyone finds out, they will run us out of here, and we'll have nothing and nobody but each other."

"Even Barbue? Even Minnie?"

"I think so," Olympia sighed. "I don't want to find out. I don't know how they see us, and I'd rather not chance it, wouldn't you agree? I'd rather be invisible, if we can; I'd rather nobody even look in our direction at all."

Diamond, though she was, to anyone's eye, the bigger and broader and more able to defend herself, was the more frightened. She hunkered down into Olympia's arms.

"I don't want to be nothing," she whispered as Olympia pressed her face to her neck. Diamond was shaking.

"You will never be nothing to me," Olympia kissed along the tender warmth, "and that is all that matters." She could feel Diamond sigh and shiver at the touch of her mouth, and Olympia trembled with a rush of power she'd never felt before.

"No, not to you," Diamond whispered, attempting to straighten up and away from Olympia, but failing to pull herself far enough from the kisses. "I mean really being gone, turning to nothing, disappearing like everybody else. I've already lost my baby and my family; I don't want to lose myself as well."

Olympia stopped and thought. "Well, I can still see you and I'll be your family. And Barbue and Minnie and Ramus will, too. You're still warm and real to all of us. Nothing has happened."

"Yet." Diamond said this and pushed Olympia back to look in her eyes. "It happens without warning. We don't know why. It's happening to everyone, like the world is just swallowing us all up."

"I've been disappearing all my life. It's really not so bad, being invisible to most people. You can get away with a lot when nobody sees you. It can sometimes be a good thing."

"Everybody else isn't like you. They're not invisible, they're *going somewhere*. It might be somewhere wonderful, or it could be awful, but they're no longer *here*. Nobody knows who's going next, or why, or where. It's as if they just stop *existing*."

"I think as long as you matter to someone, you won't disappear," Olympia whispered. She pressed her mouth again to Diamond's neck, and Diamond, despite herself, sighed and shivered.

"Robin went, and Barbue loved him beyond reason," she said. "People cared about Arnold and Sarah, if not the others."

"Not the others, not the Mirnovs," Olympia said. "And nobody liked Magnus."

"But he mattered. We're lost without him, no matter how much we all disliked him. And I'm sure the crew had people who loved them. They loved each other. So did the Mirnovs."

"I love—" Olympia started, then shook her head, thinking better of it. The last time she'd said the words she was about to say to Diamond, it had been a disaster. She changed course. "I am not going to disappear." She said this firmly, wrapping her arms tighter around Diamond's waist.

"Promise me that."

"I am not going to disappear."

What Olympia forgot was that Diamond still wore the costume, and her waist was covered in fine glass chips so that it sparkled. It felt, usually, and to the casual touch, only rough as a cat's tongue, but dragging her bare arms across it was another thing. When Diamond wriggled away and Olympia opened her arms, they were raw and red, dotted here and there with blood.

*   *   *

ONCE THE FLYING MIRNOV FAMILY had disappeared, what circus remained was pitifully small: Aside from Olympia and Diamond, there were Samu and his bear Viselik, the merman and mermaid pair of lovers Vittorio and Giovanna, Blank the Living Book, the little troupe of clowns, Ramus, Minnie, and Madame Barbue. Since the only performers who used the main tent were Olympia, Samu, and the troupe of clowns, everyone decided it was best to shut it down and only keep the sideshow going; Samu could easily move his act to the smaller tent, as could the clowns. It meant a much quicker setup and strike down, so it also meant less work and less time between stops. They needed this, because all the absences also meant a good deal less money.

With the move to the sideshow tent, however, there was no wire for Olympia to walk. After the disaster with the Mirnov Family, Olympia refused to walk a wire that hadn't been correctly set up by proper riggers. She switched to something far less dangerous and became a sideshow act called Nova the Half Man, which followed Barbue's performance.

As Nova, Olympia wore a costume that was on one side a man's morning suit and on the other a frilled, hooped, old-fashioned dress that reached to the ground. On one side, she wore half of a man's bowler hat, slicked her hair back, and even went so far as to carefully pencil on half a moustache. On the other, she wore her hair loose under half of a fashionable lady's hat, which swooped around her cheek in layers of tulle and silk flowers and ribbons, so ornate as to be nearly ridiculous. Out of one corner of her mouth, she dangled an unlit cigarette. The opposite cheek, she heavily rouged. With all her training in balance and physical control, it was a good project to try, with one half meant to move in graceful, small circles and the other half meant to command space with sweeping, open-legged strides.

She had little to do but stand there, chewing on the cigarette dangling from one corner of her mouth, boldly ogling the women with one eye while trying to smile shyly at the men with the other half of her face. She presented herself first in silhouette from the feminine side, singing a song from *Naughty Marietta*—a duet between a man who dreamt of being something greater than he was and a woman who offered her sympathy. She turned back and forth to showcase each side of her character and sing each part of the duet—as Simon, she dreamed of being a swashbuckling pirate and, as Lizette, she flitted in vapid musical pity. Sometimes she became confused as to whether her voice should be high and feminine or low and masculine—mostly because Lizette didn't sing of any dreams of her own and this seemed terribly wrong to Olympia—and so sometimes the wrong voice came out of the wrong side, and her gentleman's side sang the lady's warbling accompaniment, or her lady's side sang with a deep, rough voice about being a buccaneer. But it only seemed to add to the comedy of the show, and the crowd adored it when she got it backward. She began to incorporate those slips intentionally, producing something closer to a bawdy cabaret act starring what the audience saw as a strange, mixed-up creature whom everyone began calling Naughty Nova.

Olympia loved performing as Nova—she stayed completely solid and visible without worry, and her skin felt right, as if she'd pulled off her clothing and dived into a cool lake, that clean and that perfect. It was like standing nude in front of a wildly applauding audience. It was like finally breathing air after holding her breath. Becoming Nova wasn't so much an act of putting something *on* as it was an act of peeling off the heavy, hot layers that muffled and hid Nova away. Oddly, it was only by taking layers *off* that she became more solid, more present and real.

Diamond watched every performance from the side of the stage, and laughed and cheered along with the crowd, though this did not seem so much for support, but rather that she could not contain her own enthusiasm when Olympia performed as Nova. On Nova's first night onstage, after the performances were finished and the audience gone, Diamond clasped Olympia's wrist tightly and dragged her to her trailer—still in costume and makeup and with sweat clinging to the matted underside of her hair—and showed her, in no uncertain terms and in ways she'd never used before, how much she approved of the performance. Olympia found that she loved to wear the pants (half of them, anyway) and the vest and the penciled-on moustache and that she loved to play the ardent suitor to Diamond's shyer, lacier self. After every performance, they retired quickly to Diamond's trailer and, before long, everyone was suspicious and a few people had guessed that they were lovers.

"Come walk with me," Minnie said to Olympia, holding out her hand one evening after dinner. Olympia looked at her blankly, a little afraid.

"I promise not to bite," Minnie said. "I've already eaten."

From the long table, Barbue and Ramus watched them carefully; Diamond looked pale.

With less fuss than she felt like making, Olympia went. She knew that if she made objections, suspicions and questions would mount. She took Minnie's offered hand and allowed her to lead her out into the dark. They walked, silently, a long way away from the tent, down to the river's edge, before Olympia gathered the courage to ask Minnie what was happening.

"That's my question for you," Minnie said. "Is something happening with you and Diamond?"

Olympia paled and dropped her hand from Minnie's, and Minnie rushed to add, "I don't ask because I want to know out of curiosity. I ask because Barbue is getting suspicious and asking questions, and she's going to come straight to you soon, and if there's something to hide from her, I'd like to know so I can help."

Olympia bit her lip and shook her head.

"You're blinking out." Minnie put her hand on her arm and squeezed. "Come back. I really do want to help you. You know, if you're in love."

"I didn't say that." Olympia could barely see her own arms and, when she held them up in a shrug, the stars, the trees, the tent and trailers all seemed to shimmer through them.

"But you are?"

"Perhaps."

Minnie inhaled a deep breath and was silent a long time.

"You know this is dangerous, if anyone finds out," she said. "You're already on the outside in the real world because of this." She waved a hand at the tent behind them. "You don't need to draw more attention to yourself and make yourself even more of a target."

"I know," Olympia said quietly.

"You must be much more discreet. Barbue already suspects, and I think many of the others do too. They won't hurt you, but they could make it hard for you to stay here."

Olympia was shocked—they'd been careful in public, and had only snuck away when nobody was watching. Happiness, apparently, made her careless.

"I'll be more discreet," she whispered, and clenched her teeth to concentrate on reappearing. She did, mostly, though a hint of starlight still burned through and the images of the tent and trailers still were faintly visible on her skin.

Minnie smiled and pulled her into an embrace. "We'll call it a Boston marriage, then. I am happy that you're in love," she whispered back. "I'm sorry that it's not with a man and that you won't have a good and proper life, but that good and proper life was probably already out of the question, since you're a sideshow girl." She smiled, then shook her head. "I mean, you're a sideshow girl-boy."

* * *

KEEPING VIGILANCE OVER HER APPEARANCE (or her lack thereof) in public had become an old habit for Olympia. It was tiring, but familiar. Now that she added to her vigilance and tried to watch her behavior around Diamond in public, however, it became terribly hard. All she wanted to do was put her hands on Diamond's waist, or kiss her neck, but she knew she could not even look at her for longer than a glance, lest she raise others' suspicions, and so she pulled back from their friendship as much as she could when they were outside their trailers. Diamond was hurt when Olympia pushed her hands away or rebuked her for paying her too much fond attention in public. In private, Olympia tried to be as loving as possible when she explained that they must be careful, that people were suspicious and were talking about the two of them already.

She could not keep herself, however, from throwing away her heavy, ugly dresses and adopting, when she was not onstage, a pair of loose trousers and a smocked shirt and vest stolen from Robin's old trunk, which Barbue had secretly entombed under her bed and was carting from town to town. She'd discovered that even the half-trousers-half-skirts she wore onstage were loads lighter and more comfortable than her dresses and permitted freer movement and less mess when she washed the crew's dinner dishes or helped to hoist the canvas into a tent. She found flat-soled boots and got rid of the white-leather heeled ones she detested but had become accustomed to wearing. She discarded her stockings and all her boned and cinched and ruffled underpinnings. And finally, last of all, she asked Diamond to help cut her long hair. In the privacy of her trailer, Diamond cropped it and slicked it with oil until it resembled Ramus's short, scruffy style. In her act, Olympia would simply adopt half a long wig—it would be easier and more convincing than greasing her long hair back anyway.

They had barely been able to finish the haircut before Diamond flung the shears aside and climbed into Olympia's lap to kiss her senseless. The less hair remained on Olympia's head, the bigger and darker her eyes looked and the more beautifully long her nose and square her jaw appeared. While Diamond was cutting and shaving her, Olympia had seen, emerging as her hair fell away, a different creature, more unearthly, more serious, and more compelling than she had been. Diamond, for her part, seemed to agree. She could not stop touching the short hair at the side of Olympia's temples, running her hands over Olympia's newly squared shoulders, or feeling the trousers.

"I'm going to call you Ol," Diamond whispered. "But just in here. Will that be all right?"

"Just in here," Olympia said.

"You're perfect, Ol." Diamond ran her hands over Olympia's head, prickling the shorter hairs at the base of her neck. "Ol," she said again, more quietly, fascinated, as if in a trance. She began to untie the shawl from around her own shoulders. "My Ol." With that, she kissed Olympia hard on the mouth and let the shawl fall.

Seven
The Disciplined Bear and His Tutor

WITH ONLY THE SIDESHOW AND no main tent, the circus was no longer a circus, but simply an Attraction (and they kept the name "The Stephens Great Attraction" because they were already known in the smaller towns through which they traveled). They left the main tent and all its riggings behind when they left Georgia; there were fewer wagons left in their caravan, and the poor horses could benefit from the easier load. The much smaller sideshow tent more easily looked filled, too, and with much smaller crowds trickling in to see the Attraction on even their biggest days, Madame Barbue and Minnie wanted to maintain at least the illusion of a full house and a successful show.

Everyone learned to do everything that needed doing, from washing dishes to rigging tents to driving wagons and mending costumes; in such a small crew, every hand was precious. Minnie took over doing the books and constantly wandered between trailers, worrying over the expense of feeding the horses, or feeding the performers, or buying even one more sequin. Somehow, though the Attraction was several times smaller, the work and the worry seemed to have multiplied several times over.

Despite all their best efforts at cutting back and shoring up, everything began to fall quickly and completely apart. Trailers hit rutted ground, lost wheels, and were abandoned empty by the roadside after their contents were consolidated into other wagons. The sideshow tent developed two new and very large rips in the canvas and, though Minnie worked to mend the tent with string and a thick needle until her fingers were red and bleeding, new tears appeared in the fabric every time it was unfurled and at last she gave up keeping it repaired and allowed it to batter itself to shreds, to become at last a great, flapping, roofless striped fringe around the performance space, barely a gesture at either decoration or shelter.

Minnie even considered, on one particularly mean day, getting rid of Samu and his bear Viselik, who ate like the quarter-ton beast he was and shat and roared and paced in his heavy iron cage, which required its own wagon, pulled by two horses specially dedicated to that purpose. But she hadn't the heart and never raised the possibility aloud.

Samu, for his part, abandoned his trailer, sold most of his belongings in Georgia, and took to sleeping and riding with his bear in the six-by-twelve-foot cage car. He was used to small spaces shared with dangerous creatures; he'd traveled to America from Hungary in the hold of a ship, smuggled with his parents and twelve hostile, hungry men who leered at his mother so threateningly, she would only sleep during the daytime when Samu and his father could watch over her. In New York, they'd lived for months in a tiny factory dormitory with so many other people that Samu barely slept and, when he did, he huddled with his parents on a pile of their belongings, lest anything be stolen or any one of them harmed as they slept.

Eventually, the whole family had moved south to Texas, where his father found work as a track repairman on the railroad and his mother served as a cook for a large and lucky family of newly rich oilmen. She would, on occasion, bring home a small portion of duck stew or a pair of slightly worn and discarded trousers that might fit either Samu or his father.

Samu had wanted to study literature and publish books—his own and those of other writers—on his own printing press, but he never made it into school. No college would take him, since he had no well-connected family or friends to recommend him, and, from every printing house and newspaper room he visited, he was turned away as soon as they saw him. "We don't hire bohunks here," too many men told him and shut door after door in his face. He worked hard to smooth out his accent so that it was barely detectable and learned to behave like a crass and entitled, wealthy young American man, but he fooled nobody; his dark eyes, his black hair, and his olive skin all spoke too loudly to anyone who looked his way.

On the stage, though, Samu could play the lofty professor with a pair of wire-rimmed glasses low on his nose, garters on his sleeves, and a book in his hand. With a stern look, Samu instructed Viselik in various activities (dancing, clapping, sitting), and then, as a finale, would read out loud a story from his book of Grimm's fairy tales, and his bear would—on cue—act out crucial parts of the story, sometimes playing the innocent, pleading child and sometimes the cruel witch or the threatening wolf. The bear was clumsy, as bears tend to be, but his act was still impressive. Offstage, Viselik, whom Samu had purchased from a group of traveling Romanians who captured and trained him as a cub, was a quiet, mild bear devoted wholeheartedly to Samu. Onstage, Samu trained him to protest with fierce roars until he was seemingly frightened into submission by the threatening crack of Samu's whip. It was the pantomime of a small man conquering a shaggy, furious mountain of a beast, and the audience loved it, especially in the eastern states, where stories about brave cowboys and untamed wilderness still seemed exotic and still won hearts.

At night, long after the audience had left the tent, littering the midway with peanut shells and crumpled, brightly colored paper wrappers, Samu and Viselik retired to Viselik's cage, where they curled together in the corner with Viselik wrapped protectively around Samu with one fat paw snug on his hip. They looked, if one squinted, like mother and cub.

* * *

IT HAD BEEN WEEKS SINCE anyone had disappeared from the Attraction, and Olympia and the others were beginning to breathe a bit easier. Even Diamond, scared as she was, started to believe the disappearances had passed, and everyone was safe again.

When Madame Barbue burst into the little clearing where the performers were sitting around a fire eating breakfast (the gathering tent and the table had been left behind to lighten the load) before the day's work began, she took everyone by surprise.

"Samu!" she shrieked. "Viselik! The bear!"

It was all anybody could get out of her, try as they might to calm her, so Ramus and Diamond and several of the clowns were dispatched to check on Samu and Viselik to see what the problem might be.

When they got to Viselik's cage, however, hoping to see man and bear curled peacefully in sleep, they found only Viselik pacing the little cage and roaring as desperately as if he had a thorn in his paw. Samu was nowhere to be found. The sun had not yet even risen, and it was gray and cold as winter. They shivered as they searched all the trailers and the sideshow tent, but Samu was gone. His clothes and all his belongings were tied in a small cloth bundle in the corner of the cage. Viselik howled pitifully and slapped the wooden floor of the car with his gigantic paws, but Samu did not come back.

"Samu is gone!" Ramus shouted when he returned to the small circle of performers gathered at the campfire.

"Impossible!" shouted one of the clowns. "He was sleeping with Viselik. I saw them lying there this morning when I came to breakfast!"

"But Samu is gone!" Ramus repeated, and the cry was taken up by several others around the fire.

"Impossible!" the first clown scoffed again, and so they all followed him to the cage, where Viselik still paced and howled. The bear had begun to claw at himself like a mourner rending his garments; Viselik's shoulders and haunches were bloodied, and tufts of matted fur skittered in the breeze over the floor of his cage.

"Samu was in there! I saw him! And there's blood!" shouted the first clown.

"It's the bear," said another clown. "I knew it would get him. The bear has eaten Samu."

"The bear has eaten Samu!" several others echoed, and it was as if the more it was repeated, the truer it became.

"Get your gun, Pollack," the first clown said to the second, shaking his head.

"No!" Olympia cried, throwing herself against the bars of the cage as if, by standing there, she could block any one of those men, even if he were holding a shotgun. "You don't know where Samu has gone! You don't know that Viselik has done this!"

"We can't take the chance that Viselik has eaten him," Ramus reasoned, as if he were speaking to a child. "If Viselik could do this to Samu, he could much more easily do it to any single one of us."

"But he hasn't!" Olympia yelled, tears streaking her face. "Look at him!"

She turned and thrust her arm out to indicate the bear, who had been thrown into such a panic by the screaming outside his cage that he was howling and thrashing more wildly than before. Quite by accident—that was clear to Olympia—Viselik lashed out with his claw and caught Olympia's arm, tearing the skin and drawing blood.

"He's gone crazy!" someone shouted.

"He's going to tear us all limb from limb!"

Panic rose, and screams, and dire predictions of Viselik's intentions, until everyone was quieted instantly when a shot clapped iron-sharp-loud and Viselik fell like a heavy tree to the floor of his cage without so much as a roar or a groan. Blood seeped into the wooden floor from the wound in his head; his face was a wreck of gore and bone, and Olympia felt she might vomit, so horrible was the sight. Diamond was at her side as quickly as she was able to push through the small group of men at the cage and she wrapped Olympia's arm in her own skirt to keep the blood from washing entirely out of Olympia's body.

"Don't look," Ramus said seriously. He gently lifted Olympia to her feet and pulled her and Diamond away from the scene by their waists.

"Viselik *didn't* eat Samu!" Olympia sobbed. "He wouldn't hurt Samu ever, not *ever*."

Olympia felt wild with grief over the bear, about whom she'd not cared one whit on the day before. Madame Barbue kissed her head over and over. Minnie took her into her own arms, rubbed her back, and whispered nonsense until Olympia could breathe properly again, but it was too late: Olympia knew she had faded, and the only evidence that she was there was the blood that her arm smeared over everything and the her-shaped space in Minnie's arms.

Between the three of them, Barbue, Minnie, and Diamond hoisted and cajoled Olympia into her trailer. They wrestled her into a chair, and Minnie set about washing and cleaning and dressing the gashes in Olympia's arm by feel, while Diamond rinsed the cloths and handed her fresh dressings, and Barbue, repeating something in French under her breath in a singsong voice entirely unlike her own, held Olympia still.

"This feels terrible," Minnie murmured, lightly pressing Olympia's torn arm, "but it will be all right; it's all right; it's fine now. Just a cut, and we can clean it, but you're only half here, darling, and you're going dim. Come back to us, darling, come back."

Diamond knelt at Olympia's side, rubbed gentle circles on her back, and whispered pleas for her to stay, to stay, to be calm and brave enough to stay visible.

Minnie washed Olympia's arm and wrapped it in clean white cloth and laid Olympia in her bed and pulled the covers high on her chest, all the while murmuring softly something soothing but senseless. She pulled the curtains closed over the trailer windows and shut the door as she led Barbue out, leaving Diamond alone with Olympia in the quiet dark. Diamond curled against Olympia's side in the cot and wrapped her arms tightly around Olympia's waist, as if nothing could pry her away.

Olympia, hurting terribly and full of deep, waterlogged exhaustion, finally safe, slipped quickly to sleep.

* * *

THE NEXT DAY, MINNIE CAME to the trailer to clean and re-dress Olympia's arm. She gently woke Olympia, but the two of them left Diamond, her hair soaked in sweat and tears and clinging to her cheeks, to sleep alone in the bed.

Minnie brought Olympia outside and carefully washed her arm with a basin of fresh water and dried it with a soft cloth.

"It looks better today," she said. "And so do you. You're less pale, and your eyes are brighter. And you're more solid now." At this last comment, she glanced up at Olympia to see her reaction, but Olympia only nodded, examining the cuts on her own arm. Minnie spread a layer of thinly sliced potatoes on the skin and wrapped a new bandage around all of it. When Olympia looked at her strangely, she smiled.

"It's a trick Ramus told me to use," she said. "Potatoes will draw out the poisons and help the wounds heal more quickly and neatly."

"It's just scratches. No poisons."

Minnie shook her head kindly and stroked Olympia's cheek. "There are poisons everywhere. There are poisons in everything."

Olympia kissed Minnie, went back into the trailer, and collapsed into the bed beside Diamond. Her arm was hot and sticky inside the bandage, despite the coolness of the potatoes and the care she took to lay it on top of the blankets, where the bandages might breathe and her arm would be safe from jostling. In her sleep, Diamond rolled to the side to make room for Olympia, pulled her close by the waist, and tucked her chin against her neck. Olympia fell back to sleep more easily than she'd ever done in her life.

They slept in Olympia's cot—without interruption from anyone—for most of the morning, until the sun had risen hot and blinding, and most of the day's work had been abandoned in favor of sitting in the shade and drinking from the flasks everyone seemed to have hidden in their pockets. When they finally woke, Olympia was disoriented and a bit dizzy with new pain. Diamond jumped to bring her fresh water and an apple, which Olympia could barely stomach but choked down as best she could, if only to get rid of the worried look on Diamond's face.

"I'm fine," Olympia told her, waving her wrapped arm to prove it.

"That bear almost tore you apart."

"He did not. He was terrified, and I got in his way. He just scratched me, and I bled."

"It was more than just a scratch," Diamond said. "You bled a lot, Ol."

"They shot him. They would have shot him no matter what I said, even if he hadn't scratched me."

"He mauled you. Maybe not on purpose, but he did," Diamond said firmly. "He didn't know how dangerous he was. He had to go."

"Viselik was a good bear," Olympia said sadly. "He was a good bear."

"He'd gone crazy with grief over Samu anyway. Nobody could have calmed him again."

At that, Olympia remembered that Samu was gone. "Viselik wouldn't have eaten Samu," she said petulantly. "I know he wouldn't."

"Ol, love, it doesn't matter now," Diamond told her.

Olympia thought that it did matter and that perhaps they should all be more worried about where Samu—and the Flying Mirnovs, and Magnus, and Arnold, and Robbie the Rubber Boy, and Dead-Eyed Susan—had gone. Whatever invisible hand was creeping in and stealing them one by one had not gone slack, but was still picking them slowly apart and had only paused for the slimmest moment, then begun again.

Instead of saying so, she lay back in her cot, with Diamond curled against her side.

"I was so worried for you." Diamond ran her fingers against the short, stiff hairs at the base of Olympia's neck. "You started to disappear."

It was clear that Diamond was trying to sound casual, but Olympia could read the panic in her voice. Her stomach dropped. She had never had to explain the condition to anyone—everyone in the circus had known her since she was a baby, and everyone just *knew*.

"That happens to me sometimes."

"What?" Diamond said, sitting up. "What happens?"

"I fade. I'm still there; I just fade, and you can see right through me."

Diamond looked at her as if she were trying to decide something. Olympia knew she sounded as if she'd lost her mind, but Diamond had seen it happen with her own eyes just the day before.

"It just happens sometimes," Olympia said helplessly. "Ever since I was a baby. Whenever I'm very... *anything*... and it doesn't matter whether I'm happy or scared or angry, I just go invisible."

"Please don't disappear," Diamond said.

"I can't help it when it happens. I can't make it start and I can't stop it, either."

"But you've never gone away like the others," Diamond ventured.

"Even if you can't see me, you can always feel me, and I can always feel everything around me. I'm still there. Just nobody sees me."

"It won't happen again. We won't let it. I'm not letting you out of my sight even once more," Diamond said without irony.

"That won't help. Nothing helps, except me not feeling too much of anything. Either I can't have real feelings, or I can't count on staying the way I am now."

Diamond curled closer against her, pressed her nose into her shoulder and sighed. "At least, with you ailing, I can stay here with you and nobody will think twice as long as I make sure everyone sees me fetch water and bandages. We can stay in here for days and days while your arm heals, and nobody will bother us at all."

Olympia closed her eyes and breathed in the beeswax smell of Diamond's hair.

"Minnie knows," Olympia mumbled sleepily, "about us."

"I figured as much," Diamond sighed, less alarmed than Olympia had imagined she would be. "It's just as well."

There was a long silence, then, and Olympia was nearly asleep when she heard Diamond sigh and say again, "It's just as well. I love you."

WHEN OLYMPIA WOKE AGAIN, IT was dark outside. She could just make out through the trailer window the faint flicker of a campfire in the distance—probably the dregs of dinner being cleaned by the evening's cooks. She languished in bed—it was empty, and Diamond was nowhere to be found, probably having gone to seek food—for as long as she could, then got up to wash the sleep from her face with the clean water Diamond had left for her in a basin on the table. Just as she was drying her neck, Diamond came bursting through the trailer door.

"Ol," she said, breathless, "I have to leave. Right now."

Olympia dropped the towel. "What? Why? What's happened?"

"This." Diamond thrust at her a letter, already opened, that was unmarked for the post and had apparently been delivered by hand. Olympia opened the envelope and pulled out the already wrinkled sheet of paper. It was thin, good paper, but the writing on it was crude: spiky black scrawls, ink seeping through to the back, holes pricked here and there by the pen nib. She read quickly the few sentences there: *I know you are there. I know you are sorry for running off. I'm coming to find you and we can be together again.*

Diamond was already grabbing the shawls she'd left lying about and stuffing them—along with any stray papers, combs, gloves, or books that her hand came across, regardless of to whom they belonged—into a canvas case.

Eight
The Half-Human Lovers

WHEN THE MAN—WHO ASKED EVERYONE to call him Tomcat whether they were speaking to him or not—showed up at the circus, he was already drunk.

He watched the shows, calling lewd remarks loudly enough that everyone near him sent dirty looks his way; the looks, however, were lost on him, as Tomcat was really quite drunk and, even if he weren't, had proven himself so stupid and boorish that sobriety would not make a bit of difference in his behavior. He persisted in heckling not only the female performers, but at all of them, even Ramus.

"Weak girlie!" he yelled when Ramus was onstage preparing to lift a heavy-looking barbell. "They should call you the Weak Baby Ray-Mouse!" He looked to his left and right, waiting for the impressed laughter of his neighbors, but they stared, stone-faced, straight ahead at the stage.

He'd come to collect his wife Louise but, upon looking for a full five minutes, hadn't found her and had instead been drawn by the advertisements for the World's Fattest Woman and the World's Strongest Man. He had, on a good and sober day, a mind as small and distractible as that of a goldfish, with just enough intellect to sustain him through regular interactions with others. This morning, however, on his walk to the traveling show where he'd heard his wife was performing as a novelty act, he'd nearly drowned himself in his flask of liquor and was, at only two o'clock in the afternoon, even looser and more dim-witted and ready to pick a fight. He'd seen the painted sign for Diamond the Danger Eater, and it was his wife's face on the buxom and leggy cartoon body, with diamonds sparkling around her waist. She looked rich, and he was going to get some of that money, even if she wouldn't come back home with him (though he hoped she would, because he was lonely and there was nothing to eat and the chores were piling up just waiting for her).

"Look at the baby, all red in the face! He's twying so haaard!" he hollered, even louder than before, just as the bright red fellow (his hair, his moustache, even his face was bright red) onstage grunted and heaved the weighted bar to his chest.

"It's fake! That barbell probably weighs as much as a stack of paper money!" Tomcat yelled. "He's got your money, the fat old crook!"

Everyone in the place turned to glare at Tomcat. Suddenly, Ramus threw the weight to the ground—the whole stage shook with it when he did—and searched the crowd with a hand over his brow.

"I'm right here, you big, orange baboon!" Tomcat yelled, waving his arms.

Everything happened at once, then: Ramus surged forward to leap off the stage and was caught and held by the bearded lady, who also had beefy arms and a red face, and a sleek-haired man and a woman who was nearly his mirror image ran directly at Tomcat from each side of the tent. They grabbed Tom's arms, ushered him roughly out of the tent, and tossed him in the dust just outside the door.

"There, now, you've got a big mouth, don't you?" the man said.

Tomcat stood up, dusted himself off, and began to stride right back to the tent door.

"Dontchya even *think* about going back in there, pal o' mine, or I can't guarantee that anyone can hold Ramus off of you again! He's the strongest man alive and he's got a redheaded temper!"

"I'm looking for Louise," he said. "My *wife!*"

At that, the man and woman both took a step back and held up their hands. The woman slunk a little behind the man and kept silent, though they both looked tough, tall and sharp-eyed and angry.

"We done nothing to your wife, pal," the man said. "And maybe you should cool off before you find her, yep? You're all steamed up. She come to the show?"

"*Louise,*" Tom emphasized with irritation. "She's *in* the show."

The two looked at him blankly.

"It's all jake, fella," the man said, smoothing the air with his hands. "We're tryna help ya."

"No Louise with us," the woman interrupted. "Maybe you should get a move on."

Tomcat held his fist; it would not turn out well if he punched that woman in front of all these people milling around, this he knew for sure. He tried again, enunciating carefully through his ginned-up slur: "Looo-eeeze. My. Wife. Is. Heeere." The woman looked at him blankly, and he could feel in the back of his hand how good it would be to haul off and crack her across her smug face.

"I'm sorry. You're mister—" the man said, stepping between Tom and the woman. His voice dangled on the air like a hook.

"Tom. Tomcat, usually," he said, extending his hand to shake. "Bowman."

"Tomcat." The man ignored Tom's hand. Distaste was clear on his face. "Mr. Bowman, I'm afraid we don't have any Louise here."

"Afraid? What are you afraid of? That's her!" he shouted and pointed at a painted sign in which Louise—more buxom and tarty than he ever knew her—held up a silver sword. Diamonds sparkled on her waist, and each wrist was wrapped in expensive-looking jeweled silver cuffs, and above her head swirled words in scarlet script he couldn't read (the script had too many flourishes and curlicues).

"That's Diamond," said the man. "And she ain't nobody's wife."

"And she's long gone by now, anyhow," the woman said, nodding. "Left early this morning."

"Twenty-three, skidoo." The man swiped the air with his hand.

"That's my wife Louise, and I come here to take her home to our baby girl," he insisted. The woman looked uncomfortable and glanced at the man; they seemed about to cave in and unfolded their arms.

"And I come to get what's mine, seeing as she's my wife, running around draped in diamonds and all that," he added and instantly knew it was a mistake. The man and woman looked at each other and refolded their arms. The woman backed up a step, but the man stepped forward.

"She's gone and she's not coming back," someone said, though Tomcat could see nobody else around.

DIAMOND HAD KISSED OLYMPIA HARD on the mouth, snapped her bag closed, slung it over her shoulder and headed for the main gate of the Attraction.

"Wait!" Olympia had called, just as Diamond was about to shut the trailer door behind her. She paused and looked back.

"You coming, too, then?" Diamond's eyes brightened.

"No, no, no—but you can't go now," Olympia said quickly. "What if you run into him when you're leaving and he's on his way here?"

Diamond stepped back inside the trailer and set her bag down. "I can't leave, because he might find me on the road, and I can't stay, because he's looking for me here. What can I do?" She looked so pained, Olympia felt her own heart rise up shaking.

"You can hide for a while in Ramus's trailer," Olympia said. "Nobody will look for you there, and if he tries to go in, Ramus can take him apart."

"You're fading out again," Diamond told her in a quiet voice.

"Never mind that. We've got bigger problems to deal with. I'll fade back in eventually; I always do."

Olympia helped Diamond slip down the line of trailers until they found the one in which Ramus lived and she shut her inside. She could hear, through the door, the faint scuff of Diamond setting her bag on the floor, and then a hard thump and a bit of whimpering as, Olympia assumed, Diamond dropped to the floor and began to cry. She put her mouth as close to the crack between the door and its jamb as she could and said in a low voice, "Everything will be fine. I'm going to find Ramus and tell him you're in there. He'll help us. You're going to be safe."

Diamond's soft sobs continued, but Olympia heard her whisper, "Thank you."

She ran to the tent where Ramus was soon to be finished onstage. She found Vittorio and Giovanna attempting to talk firmly with a very drunk, very sweaty and irate man, who was trying to press his way back into the tent, and she stood warily next to Giovanna where nobody noticed her. Vittorio stood in front of them with his feet planted far apart, as if he were already steadying himself for a blow. She tapped Giovanna on the arm and whispered, "I'm here."

Giovanna, completely unsurprised, nodded.

"I come to get what's mine!" the man shouted. "She's my wife, running around draped in diamonds!"

Before Vittorio or Giovanna could reply, Olympia stepped up to the drunk and hissed into his ear, "She's gone, and she's not coming back. Now, go!"

Tom looked startled, as if a ghost had whispered the words.

"She's my wife," he said lamely to the empty air from which the whispering seemed to have come. "I want to see her *now*."

"She's gone, and I wouldn't let her talk to such a stinking drunk even if she *were* here. Go," she growled and, feeling bold, pushed his shoulder.

The man tried to glare at Olympia, but found nobody there. He looked terrified and unsure, and then, deciding the voice had been a figment of his own addled brain, stumbled off to the line of trailers howling, "Louise! Louise!" He banged on the side of every trailer he passed until Barbue stepped into his path wielding a large wooden board and shouted, "Out!" The man—Tom—looked at her petulantly, and then yelled, "Louise!" one last time before turning on his heel and walking quickly out the main gate of the midway.

Barbue barreled up to them and dropped the wood at her feet. "Who was that man?" she demanded, shoving her fists against her hips.

"Just a drunk," Giovanna said. "We were trying to get him out. Olympia scared him, I think." She nodded at the empty-looking space where Olympia stood and raised her brows at Madame Barbue. Barbue, for her part, simply glanced at the spot where she imagined Olympia stood, huffed, and nodded approval.

"Good, girl. Good to have a spirit like you on our side. What was he screaming and banging on about?"

"He was looking for somebody," Giovanna said. "Some Louise or other. His wife."

"He wanted Diamond." Olympia knew it was best not to try to fool Madame Barbue. "He was looking for Diamond. That's her husband."

"*Putain de merde!*" Barbue cursed under her breath. "Is she in there?" She gestured to Olympia's trailer. Olympia shook her head and indicated Ramus's instead, then remembered she couldn't be seen, and said, "She's hiding in Ramus's place."

"Tell her she can come out," Madame Barbue sighed. "It's probably safe now. I think between the ghost and the screaming bearded lady, he got good and frightened off."

Olympia let herself into Ramus's trailer, where she found Diamond crouched on the floor beneath the window. She rustled papers and jostled furniture so she wouldn't startle her when she finally spoke.

After a moment of noisemaking, she told her, "He's gone."

"My god," Diamond said to her own knees. She didn't seem to know where to look when she couldn't see Olympia. "I didn't think he'd ever come for me like that. He's a drunk, and he's a terrible father, but he's too lazy to bother chasing me."

"Apparently, he's gathered up a bit of energy," Olympia said. "You're safest here, where we can watch out for him. I think he's given up and gone for good, though."

Diamond pulled herself to her feet and smacked at her legs and hips to get rid of the dust. "Ramus keeps terrible house," she muttered, swiping at the dirt that streaked her arms.

Olympia gathered Diamond's bag, pulled Diamond's arm over her own, and said, "You're going to move in with me. Madame Barbue can move into your bunk." At Diamond's stricken look, she said, "It's the safest thing. Everyone will understand."

"Not that," Diamond said. "You're just getting solid again. I can't see you all the way, but I see bits of you. It's strange."

"You'll get used to it. Unfortunately."

Diamond let her hand go limp against Olympia's arm and followed her out of Ramus's trailer and down the caravan line until they got to Olympia's door. Olympia bent and tried to scoop Diamond up to carry her inside, but Diamond backed away and planted herself firmly.

"Absolutely not," she said. "I can walk on my own."

"I thought—" Olympia started, but Diamond began to climb up the stairs and reached behind her to pull Olympia along by the hand.

"I can get there on my own steam. It doesn't mean I don't want you around, just because I don't need you to carry me."

Once they were safely inside Olympia's trailer, Diamond closed and locked the door behind them. She was grimy; her skin felt slick and gritty at the same time.

"I want to keep you near me," Olympia said, "so I can make sure he doesn't come back for you."

Outside, they could hear dim noises: the crowd's burbling, the distant clang of the bell on the strength-testing machine, and the choppy patter of Madame Barbue, who was acting as a stand-in barker for the sideshow, calling out to passersby in her hoarse, clipped English. Olympia drew the curtains more tightly closed, then put her arms around Diamond, heedless of the grime and Diamond's protests that she was filthy. She kissed her mouth until Diamond stopped making irritated noises and began to kiss her back. Only then did Olympia step back.

Diamond slipped her arms around Olympia's waist, pulled her close again and pressed her nose into the crook of her neck. "You only want me near to keep an eye out? Only for that, Ol?"

"No," Olympia whispered. "Not only for that."

*   *   *

THERE WERE TWO KINDS OF people on the midway: the rubes, who truly and wholeheartedly believed in everything they saw, and the wisenheimers, who understood that everything they saw was most likely a hoax, but loved the show for just that reason.

Vittorio and Giovanna Visco had seen both kinds of people— endless streams of each—walk past their tank, and they respected neither. The tank—a large glass-and-wood structure filled with water— was set up just outside the sideshow tent, so that passersby were drawn to it by natural curiosity, and then into the tent by default. It was a bit seedy: Vittorio wore only a long, sea-green wrap to hide his legs and approximate a finned tail, and his chest was entirely bare. Giovanna wore the same wrap around her legs, and a top made of seashells and green ribbons meant to suggest seaweed that covered only a small portion of her body. There was no show—they simply floated there, together, in the water. They spent so much time in the tank that their skin was pale and wrinkled.

When the crowd was big enough, or when they were trying to attract the single men who wandered the grounds alone, a bit drunk and rowdy and looking for a glimpse of something salacious (a thigh, a bared back or neck), they would play like lovers and kiss passionately until the crowd clapped. At other times, Giovanna would float to the front of the tank, letting her loose hair curl seductively in the water, and Vittorio would float in the background and try to be unobtrusive. It all depended on the mood of the midway, which the two had learned to read as easily as they'd learned to hold their breath and breathe sporadically from the underwater air tank: it was not difficult, but took a bit of initial practice to get right.

They had gone with their parents directly from Sicily to Bensonhurst in Brooklyn. Giovanna had been sent to work in a factory where she sewed buttons onto ladies' boots, and Vittorio was put to work in a slaughterhouse, slicing and wrapping freshly killed meat. When Giovanna came home one day and tearfully showed him her bloodied, wrapped hand—she had, due to cross-eyed exhaustion, pushed a leather needle straight through her own finger—Vittorio promised her she would never go back. The very next day, the two snuck off to see the sideshow at Dreamland in Coney Island and afterward they proposed their own act to the owner. Giovanna sewed their costumes, and Vittorio built a tank and hid a breathing tube behind a clutch of seaweed. They entered the tank one week later as Vittorio and Giovanna, the Half-Human Lovers.

When a man came by their tank to offer them living quarters and a good salary—enough to send a bit home each week—if they would leave Dreamland and perform as the mermaid and merman in his traveling circus and sideshow, they took it. Steel-hearted, they packed their bags as their father and mother sobbed and begged them not to go; they left anyway, and within a week, they were far from New York, with a trailer and a weekly salary of their own, and a freshly built tank with their names glittering at the top. Less than one year later, their mother wrote to them with the news that Dreamland had burned to the ground.

*   *   *

SINCE THE RIGGING CREW HAD disappeared, Vittorio and Giovanna had learned to set up and fill their own tank. It was bulky and heavy, and even unfilled it took two horses to pull it alone—no other cages or equipment, not even a tent's weight, could be added to the wagon that carried it. Filling the tank was an arduous task that took hours and the help of nearly everyone left. They had to set up, always, close to a river (in all fairness, the group needed to do this anyway to ensure that there was enough water for drinking and cooking and washing), and buckets were, one by one, carried from the river and emptied into the tank until it was full.

Once the tank was filled with water, Vittorio and Giovanna spent another long hour dressing it with the ribboned seaweed and rocks they carried for just such purpose. Then they retired for several hours to the trailer they shared. There were rumors among the Attraction performers that Vittorio and Giovanna, despite being brother and sister, really were lovers and not just pretending for the show, and not one of the performers had ever been invited into their trailer. Nobody could figure out what the two were doing during the hours spent hidden alone together, those hours between setting up their tank and beginning their show. Minnie had once tried to speak to Giovanna about it, tried to wheedle an invitation inside their room to see, at least, where they lived, but Giovanna was a quiet woman who shied away from speaking with anyone but her brother and was certainly not about to invite someone in for tea.

When Giovanna and Vittorio still had not emerged from their trailer a full hour after the midway had opened, Barbue began to worry. She had taken up her place in front of the sideshow tent to begin her bark, luring everyone into the tent for the show. Giovanna and Vittorio would perform their show afterward, but their presence in the tank before the tent show helped to pull in the rubes. They were, however, nowhere in sight.

"They're gone, too," she said to Minnie, who stood with her as a lure outside the tent. "Like the rest. They're gone."

"Don't worry. They've probably just slept too long and now they can't come walking out here in front of everyone, can they? They'll have to be snuck in somehow."

Minnie had a point—they couldn't just come hobbling over in their fish tails in front of everyone. Even the most gullible rubes would see through that. Barbue steeled herself and waited until the show had started, but there was no sign of them. By the time she'd finished her own act (pulling her beard, smoking her cigar, twirling her parasol), they still had not showed up. The crowd spilled out of the tent and down the midway with only a few curious and disappointed glances at the tank as they went. A tickle of worry wormed through Barbue's gut and up her throat, but she swallowed it back, knowing her own tendency to panic before it was truly warranted. But by the time the sky had blackened and the lamps were lit, Giovanna and Vittorio still had not appeared, and Barbue knew they were gone for good.

No one, least of all Diamond, expected Tom to reappear during her show late that afternoon, but that is exactly what happened. Somehow he slipped in, despite all of Madame Barbue's careful warnings to everyone to keep him out, and he stood at the back of the crowd, yowling—he was far drunker than when he'd left earlier—through the entire show. He would have made more trouble during Diamond's act, but Barbue and Ramus stood nearby and glared darkly in his direction to keep him quiet.

After the show, however, he pushed his way through the crowd.

"Louise!" he bellowed. "Looo-eeeze, goddamn it!"

Diamond, who had been removing her boots, sighed heavily and stood to walk barefoot to the rows of benches where Tom was howling her name. She shook her head at where she knew Olympia was standing, but Olympia followed her out anyway—invisible—without Diamond knowing or protesting. Several of the other performers followed, too.

"Tom, I'm here. What do you want?" Diamond said flatly.

"Tomcat!" the man hissed.

"Tomcat," Diamond sighed. "What do you want?"

"Yer comin' along with me, now. Enough of this."

"I'm not leaving. I have a job here." Diamond folded her arms across her chest. Olympia pressed against her side, and out of the corner of her eye she could see Minnie and Barbue whispering to Ramus; the three of them hovered close.

"Enough of this," Tom said, as if he'd run out of ideas.

"Where's Dahlia?"

Tom ignored the question, but lunged toward Diamond, his hands outstretched. She stepped back before he could put his hands on her hips, and he teetered and lost his balance.

"I asked you: Where's Dahlia?" Diamond demanded.

"She's a-right," Tom slurred. "She's a-right, for having her mother run out on her. I put her with Peggy n' Sam."

"You put her with…" Diamond trailed off, though her voice rose in panic. "She's with your sister? She's in Virginia?"

"They took 'er 'cause I couldn't, and they don't got kids, and without you I just couldn't…" Tom started to cry and swatted furiously at the tears, as if he were more surprised than anyone by their appearance. Diamond, at the sight of this, lunged at Tom. Olympia put her hand on Diamond's arm to stop her, but Diamond was hard and focused, and shook her off.

"How *could* you?" she roared, rattling him by the shoulders. Everyone in the tent took a step back except Tom, who seemed oblivious. "You sent Dahlia away? She's just a child! She's *your* child!"

"Had to," Tom mumbled. "Couldn't do it without you there."

"Your sister and her husband are idiots!" Diamond screamed. At that, Tom stood, straightened, and swung his fist in the air. He swung wide and missed Diamond's jaw.

"Whoa, there." Ramus put his arms around Tom to keep him from swinging again. Tom sagged in his arms and looked pleadingly at Diamond.

"If you come back with me, we could bring 'er home again. She needs her mother, Louise."

Ramus let him go and stepped back warily, though he made it apparent that he was still watching him. Tom sounded nearly reasonable to Diamond, though she knew that voice too well to believe it. It was oily and wheedling and it turned her stomach. He fell forward again. This time no one was at the ready, and he managed to hook onto one of Diamond's wrists. She twisted her arm, but could not pry it loose from his grip. "Come away from this," he growled, waving a loose arm to indicate Ramus, the tent, the trailers, and, though he didn't know it, Olympia. "You look like a whore. Come home with me, and we can bring Dahlia home."

"Diamond, no," Olympia said, trying to push herself between Tomcat and Diamond so that her beloved would feel her support.

"If we go, you'll help bring Dahlia back home, and she'll stay with us?" Diamond asked Tom, looking directly through the space where Olympia stood.

"Promise," Tom said. "Whatever you want, Louise, we can leave her there or bring her home."

"I would never leave her." Diamond was leaning toward Tom with her arm outstretched. "Swear it, she'll come home."

"I swear it," Tom slurred. "Just as soon as you and I are right again, maybe a month, we'll get Dahlia home."

"What? No! We have to bring her home right away!"

"It won't be no good that way," Tom said. "You and I need to get right first. With Dahlia there, we won't have a chance. We need time to see things straight, just you and me."

"I'm not coming home for you," she cried. "I'm coming home for Dahlia."

"Aren't two ways," Tom said. "You come home to both of us or you don't come home at all."

Olympia put her arm around Diamond's waist and pulled her close against her hip to hiss in her ear, "You will *not* go. We will get Dahlia without him." Diamond looked hopeful for one moment, before her face fell.

"She's with his sister," she whispered to the space where she knew Olympia was standing. "That witch won't ever give her back unless Tom says to do it." Diamond pulled herself away from Olympia and stood as strong as she could, facing Tom. "I can't go with you," she said. "No matter what. I want to take Dahlia by myself if you won't have her."

"A girl needs a mother *and* a father and a stable home. Not some whore and her traveling circus." He eyed the crowd of performers that had begun to gather. Olympia bristled at his glare but shook herself, knowing the look was not for her—he couldn't even see her.

"I can't," Diamond said again and turned to walk away to her trailer.

Before anyone could think, Tom growled, "You're coming with me," and grabbed Diamond's arm. He yanked her backward, then turned and walked, without stopping or even slowing down to let Diamond catch herself from stumbling, to the line of trees just outside the midway.

Olympia ran after them, screaming, "Let her go!" But before she'd run four steps, Ramus flung himself violently toward her voice and, on the third try, knocked her to the ground. "Stay!" he told her. "You'll get hurt!"

Ramus scrabbled up and ran past her then, following the trail of Tom and Diamond into the trees. Olympia got to her feet and went running, followed closely by Minnie, with Barbue huffing along a few yards behind them. By the time Olympia caught up with Tom, he had Diamond pressed up against a tree and was hissing something in her ear. It must have been terrible, what he said, because her face looked as if she were about to rip in half. He held her hand by the wrist against the tree above her head, his arm leaned clear across her windpipe, and he gripped and pressed so tightly that both her hand and her face were bright red.

"Get off her," Olympia shouted, running at Tom, who looked around wildly to find the source of the shout. He began to fling his free arm in large arcs around his body, screaming, "Get away! You've got no business here! Evil spirit! You're nothing!"

Olympia dodged his arm and lost her balance; she fell over a tree root and went down. She didn't bother to get back up, but scrambled on hands and knees toward Tom and Diamond.

"Diamond!" she hissed until Diamond made a small choking noise, which only made Tom press harder and whisper, "Shut up!"

Before Olympia could do or say anything in response, Ramus had flung himself at Tom and torn him off Diamond. Diamond fell back, coughing and red. Olympia scuttled forward, pulled herself up by the nearest tree, and rubbed soothing circles on Diamond's back as Minnie and Barbue bent with her, trying to help her breathe. When Olympia heard thumps and an ugly gurgling noise and looked up, she saw Ramus standing over Tom, who lay on his side with his face a bloody mess of meat. Ramus kicked him with his boot heel, then brought his fist down on the side of Tom's face, over and over.

"No! You're killing him!" Minnie screamed and pulled Ramus back. As soon as he felt her hands on him, Ramus stopped punching, stopped moving, went limp. He let Minnie pull him back and force him to sit in the leafy damp. Minnie, tear-streaked, hummed and babbled, trying to wipe Ramus's bloody fists in her skirt. Tom lay still and silent, finally, oozing blood. Barbue leaned over him for a long time, holding her wrist near his mouth and then pressing her cheek to his chest. Finally, she sat up.

"It's done," she told Ramus. "We need to dig a hole."

"He's dead?" Diamond gasped.

"Get her out of here," Barbue growled in Olympia's direction. To Diamond, she said, her voice lighter and kinder, as if she were speaking to a child, "Diamond, my sweetness, go with Olympia back to your trailer. You need to bathe and tend to those cuts and bruises he put on you and then you need to rest. Go back to camp, Diamond. Go with Olympia."

Olympia held out her hand, and Diamond glanced down and took it.

"You're shimmering in," she said in wonder. "I can see just a little of you now. You're coming back." She hid her face in the crook of Olympia's neck.

"It'll be right again. We'll get you clean, we'll pack up, and we'll go get Dahlia and bring her back here with us," Olympia said, knowing she was lying. But Diamond looked hopeful and began to walk.

"She's a quick learner," she said. "She can learn high-wire, or maybe tumbling, or how to fit herself in a tiny box."

"It'll be right again," Olympia said once more and steered Diamond back to the trailers.

RAMUS, MADAME BARBUE, AND MINNIE buried Tomcat in the woods and never spoke of it again.

Nine
The Strongest Person Alive

OLYMPIA LED DIAMOND OUT OF the woods and to her trailer. Every step homeward made Olympia more solid; she could feel it. Without a word, she pulled Diamond up the few trailer steps and inside. Barbue, if she had an ounce of compassion—and Olympia knew she did—would stay at Minnie's place and leave the two of them alone.

Olympia closed the door behind her. Diamond was shaking and hollow-eyed.

"He killed him," Diamond said. "Ramus killed Tomcat."

"No," Olympia said firmly and began to comb Diamond's hair with her fingers. "You need to get to bed, and for that, you need to change your clothes and wash up. Ramus didn't do anything."

"He did, I saw him do it, he kicked—"

"No," Olympia insisted. "Ramus did nothing. You didn't see anything. You saw Ramus chase him into the woods after that man tried to beat the life out of you in front of everyone, and then we came back here and got you into bed."

"But I saw—" Diamond tried again, before Olympia had pushed her back against the door.

"You can't trust what you see. Half the time, you can't see me, but you know I'm there. You can't trust what you think you saw," she said slowly. "You didn't go into the woods. We came here." She looked at

Diamond so hard it made her eyes hurt and she shook her head very slightly. Diamond was clear-eyed and, at once, nodded.

"You're right. I probably imagined those things."

"You probably did." Olympia ran her fingers lightly across Diamond's throat. "He got you real good. Does it hurt?"

"It's okay. My voice just hurts when I talk."

"Stop talking, now," Olympia soothed. She slowly unbuttoned Diamond's costume and pulled it from her. She rolled her stockings down and off; they were dirty and torn to shreds, and Olympia wadded them up to throw away.

"Your stockings are ruined," she said. "Where are your shoes?"

"I think I took them off in the tent before everything—before everything happened. I think I left them there."

"You went all that way in just stockings?" Olympia gasped, touching Diamond's raw-looking feet. She filled a basin with water from the pitcher at the bedside, then knelt again at Diamond's feet and began to wash the blood and dirt carefully away with her hands. "My god, your feet are all slashed," she whispered.

"I was running in the woods," Diamond said blankly.

"No, you were never in the woods," Olympia said. "You were practicing without your shoes in the tent, and the wood floor cut you up terribly. Remember that?"

"That's right," Diamond said, as if she were just remembering.

* * *

ONCE RAMUS HAD USED a snapped-off tree branch to dig a hole in the soft ground by the river, once he and Barbue had rolled Tom into it and Minnie had helped him to press the earth into place over the body, once Minnie and Barbue had slinked off to the trailers arm in arm with Barbue weeping softly on Minnie's shoulder as they went, only then was Ramus left alone.

He stood by himself on the riverbank in the dark for a long while, letting the water rush over his boots and wash away the blood and hair that had stuck to them. He cleaned his hands, which were caked with mud, in the river's shallows and dried them on his pants, then turned and walked slowly to his trailer. When he had closed the door, he peeled back his suspenders and let his pants and shirt drop to the floor, then scrubbed his face and chest with a wet rag until the skin glowed pink. He poured himself a glass of whiskey from the flask he kept hidden in a cupboard by his bunk and sat on the edge of the cot and drank.

It was true that if he had not punched Tomcat, if he had not killed him, then Tomcat would have killed Diamond that very night in front of all of them, or else he would have come for her again and again until he did kill her. It was also true that Ramus had kicked and punched the man until his face was a sickening mess of oozing flesh, and that he had done it before he realized he intended to. He *had* intended to kill him, that was for sure, but he'd also slipped into a curdled rage at the sight of the man's arm across Diamond's throat, and hadn't known how to stop himself. No one else had stopped him, either, but that hardly mattered now; a man's actions were his own responsibility, and there was no way to undo or apologize for what had been done. When they dumped Tomcat's body into the hole Ramus dug, the man hadn't even resembled a person anymore, he was so bloody and ripped apart.

Ramus finished the whiskey in his glass and then drank straight from the flask. He drank until he vomited, wiped his mouth, and then drank again. There was no pleasure in it, and no relief—it burned and made him feel nauseated and too full and as if he were spinning, and still he drank until, finally, the room went black.

WHEN AT LAST SHE WOKE, long after Olympia had kissed her calm and the two had curled together in her overheated bunk and slipped into sleep, Diamond felt much better. Tom was gone, and he wasn't ever going to look for her again. It was as if someone had just unbound her hands from behind her back for the first time in years: She could move again, and breathe right, and she felt free.

This much was better, but Dahlia, she knew, was still out there, somewhere in Virginia with a woman and a man whom Diamond neither liked nor trusted. Tom's sister and her husband were selfish and cruel people; they'd once had a daughter of their own, but the girl died while she was still a baby. Diamond had only heard the story from Tom and so she couldn't decide whether the baby's death had made the couple as nasty as they were, or whether their callowness and cruelty was the cause of their baby's death in the first place.

It mattered little because the two were awful people, and they had their claws sunk into Dahlia, and Diamond didn't want her daughter anywhere near them. She tugged her boots on over her bare, raw feet and was just splashing her face with water from the basin when Olympia rolled over and looked at her.

"Where are you going?" she said.

"Dahlia. He left Dahlia with that monster sister and brother-in-law of his, and I have to go get her back."

Olympia stood, shook her head, reached for Diamond, and pulled her in.

"We can't ever do that," Olympia said sadly. When Diamond looked at her, betrayal hard on her features, Olympia sighed and said, "We can never get your daughter now, because when Tom goes missing, the first person the police will want to talk to is you. They'll never let Dahlia be with you, ever, and she might end up with a dead father *and* a dead mother. And if not, if you stay alive, you will always have to run, and Dahlia will always have to run with you. You need to stay far away, for Dahlia's sake and yours."

Diamond looked as if she would break in half, but simply nodded and wilted. She allowed Olympia to peel off her clothes, bathe her gently, pull a fresh dressing gown over her head, and put her to bed. Olympia slouched into a chair at Diamond's bedside and fell asleep with her head on her arms. Diamond stayed awake long into the night, but she did not cry.

*   *   *

THOUGH MAGNUS WAS GONE AND nobody was pushing her to do it, Diamond got back onstage the next day. She was drunk when she did it, and dangerously sloppy; in the past she had been careful with the sword, but now she brandished it above her head and thrust it down her throat with such force it was a wonder it didn't keep going and slide out her stomach. With gleeful eyes, she performed in next to nothing at all—she'd torn her costume in half so that her breasts spilled out and her entire belly was exposed, and the audience could see the ripple of her stomach as she took in the chain or the sword or the fire. She refused to perform in stockings or shoes, but left her legs bare. She added to the act—chewed glass and swallowed nails—and left the mice out entirely.

Two weeks passed, and the circus stayed where it was; everyone was too tired, too broken and too discouraged to move it to the next town, even though audiences were thinning and worry was building. This only emboldened Diamond, as the crowds that did come were men who'd been before and were now already drunk by noon, staggering into the tent and yelling insults at the performers until Diamond came out. Then the tent filled with whistles and catcalls as she sulked across the stage, threw her head back, and slid a sword down her throat. She did this so imprecisely that, more often than not, the corners of her mouth were cut and bleeding at the end of the day. Her act was moved to the last spot in the show's rotation, because the crowd got so rowdy and nasty when she left the stage nobody could follow her. She was reckless and loose, uninterested in Olympia, the Attraction, the size of the crowds, or even her own safety.

The more dangerous her act became, the more her audience grew.

When she left the stage each night, Diamond walked to her trailer to eat alone, locking the door so that neither Minnie nor anyone else could get in. She ate little and drank heavily from a store of bottles she kept stashed in cupboards and under chairs all over the trailer. Every evening, she sat in the same chair and scrawled the same sloppy letters to Dahlia, over and over again: *Mama loves you so much. I miss you. I hope you grow up strong.* When she finished one letter, she folded it up carefully, slid it under her pillow, and started writing the next. While she slept, the letters slid out and skittered across the floor. In the morning, as she shuffled to the basin to clean her face, she kicked them without seeing; they piled up under the cots and chairs and in the corners of the room. Within weeks, the trailer was choked with great, teetering heaps of her scrawled wishes, and there was not an inch of space from which they didn't spill.

* * *

OLYMPIA TRUSTED VERY FEW PEOPLE in the world; the list had, in recent weeks, dwindled to just one name: Minnie. Barbue had gone mad when Robin disappeared and, though she'd recovered a bit, was never quite the same. Diamond had lost her senses when she realized she'd lost Dahlia forever, and now Ramus was crumbling. Only Minnie was steadfast. Though she'd watched Ramus kill Tomcat and had helped to bury him, she was stalwart in her sanity; she grieved for everyone who was lost to the Attraction, but she still cared vehemently for those who remained.

At dinners, Ramus was silent and unkempt. He shoveled food in his mouth as quickly as he could, and ate very little—eating was a mechanical inconvenience that held no pleasure and, on most nights, represented only the slightest self-sustaining gesture. Immediately after he scraped the scraps off his plate and slid it into the soapy bin to be washed, he left the campfire and retired to his trailer, from which he did not emerge until it was time to work in the morning. He spoke to nobody and, if anyone spoke to him, even Barbue or Minnie, he would simply grunt and avert his eyes.

He grew frighteningly thin as the weeks passed; his muscles sagged and his eyes became black and still and entirely unlit. Soon, he was too weak to lift his barbells and he stopped performing. Soon after that, he became too weak even to lift his own arms. Nobody knew what to make of his illness, but most of the remaining performers stayed far from his trailer, worrying that it might be consumption or something equally awful and contagious. He stayed in bed and slept and only ate or drank when Barbue or Minnie brought him something and held the spoon to force it into his mouth.

Ramus was, by the end of just a few weeks, pale and thin and silent, faded until he was practically indistinguishable from the sheets he lay on. His hair, still fire red, was the only thing that gave away his presence.

"Poor Ramus," Minnie said one afternoon, stroking his cheek as he lay in bed and stared past her. She'd already given up getting him to eat and had left the bowl and spoon on the floor by her feet. Ramus barely moved, though his eyes shifted to meet hers. They were pleading.

"I don't know what you want, poor Ramus," Minnie whispered. "Just tell me and I'll do it for you." She picked up his hand and squeezed. "Squeeze back, love, and let me know you're there."

But Ramus's hand was limp in hers; when she let it drop onto the bed, he lay still and closed his eyes.

Minnie visited Ramus in his trailer every evening. Barbue went in the mornings, and during the day Ramus slept. He had become, so quickly, such a pale and wasted version of himself that Olympia could not bring herself to see him at all.

On the sixth morning of his illness, however, Minnie pulled Olympia aside after the early chores.

"You must come see Ramus soon," she said quietly.

"I can't," Olympia said. "I've got a basket of mending to do today and then I was going to go try to catch some fish so we're not short on food again."

But Minnie shook her head and tightened her grip on Olympia's arm. "No. You must come see Ramus *today.*"

Minnie looked seriously into Olympia's eyes; each time Olympia tried to move to break the look, Minnie squeezed her arm and jerked her until she looked up again. "*Today,* Olympia, no matter how much you don't want to go. He saved Diamond's life with Tomcat, and he's always protected you. And now he needs you, even if he can't tell you that. Don't be cruel to him, not now."

Olympia looked at the broom with which she'd been sweeping the bits of paper and peanuts off the floor of the tent. "I can't, Minnie. I just can't look at him like that. He doesn't look like Ramus anymore and he won't even talk. His eyes look like there's nobody in his head."

"Doesn't matter how much it scares you," Minnie said, "because he's there. I can feel it. He's inside his head and he can't get out and he needs the people who have always loved him to keep loving him."

"I do love him," Olympia protested.

"Then you need to come visit him. It will do him good," Minnie said, and then looked pointedly at Olympia. "And you."

"It's only going to hurt me more."

Minnie looked at Olympia for a very long, still moment. Her face was fiercely angry. She narrowed her eyes and shook her head slowly.

"Don't leave him now; he's never once left you when you needed him."

"He's left now," Olympia whispered. "He's gone."

"He's *not,*" Minnie insisted. "But I think he's dying."

Olympia had never once seen Minnie cry—she had been a substitute mother since her own mother had disappeared, and, with the blindness that children often willingly assume, Olympia had only ever read love or anger on her face. Now mixed with that love and anger were fear and sorrow and a stony determination.

Olympia nodded and tried to swallow the strangled feeling in her throat.

She went to Ramus's trailer, but lasted only ten minutes by his side before she burst into tears and left again. Ramus lay under the sheets, staring silently at the ceiling. Not an ounce of fat or muscle was left on his body; his skin was lifeless and dull, as if it were a piece of cotton draped over the pile of his bones. His beard, still red but no longer stiff and carefully trimmed, wilted in matted curls on his slack jaw.

"I'll bring a razor tomorrow and clean up your beard," Olympia tried. "Minnie doesn't know how, and it's gone untamed too long. It looks like a bright red tumbleweed happened to land on your chin."

Ramus's eyes didn't move; he didn't react at all.

"I miss you," she tried again. "And Diamond misses you. You saved her life. The circus is falling apart without you, too. Please come back, Ramus."

Ramus closed his eyes and let his head fall to the side, a gesture which Olympia decided might be understood as an acknowledgement.

"You can hear me," she told him. Ramus's eyes remained closed. Olympia squeezed his hand, wincing when the bones seemed to crack and fold from the gentlest pressure.

"Please, Ramus," she said. "You can hear me."

WITHOUT DISCUSSION OR EVEN A clear moment of decision, Minnie moved her belongings into Madame Barbue's trailer and Olympia brought her things—one bag of clothing, a pair of shoes, and an armload of books—to Diamond's place and took over Minnie's cot, though that was simply for appearances. It should have been a joyous occasion, at least for Olympia and Diamond, but it wasn't. Minnie had moved to be closer to Barbue, so that they could make sure at least one of them sat with Ramus at all times, and Diamond and Olympia had shifted to accommodate the change. The fact that it pleased them very much to do so, even as Ramus wasted away into nothing and Barbue and Minnie were beside themselves with grief, was a guilty secret they kept carefully between them.

* * *

AFTER TWO MORE WEEKS, THERE had been no improvement in Ramus's condition. He'd gone from muscled to thin to skeletal and could hardly lift his own head to drink the water Barbue tipped into his mouth. He slept most of the day and night, only stirring when shaken awake by Barbue or Minnie, and even then only keeping his eyes open under protest—at least, they were fairly certain Ramus was protesting, though the only indication was a slight glare in his eyes. Barbue took every opportunity to rile him, because at least it produced a spark—however brief—of the old Ramus. She tried giving him awful news (mostly lies) about the well-being of the circus, about Minnie, or Olympia, and it worked a couple of times—a brief but clear look of anger or worry shot through his eyes—but the more often she tried the trick, the more frequently it failed to have effect. Either he no longer trusted Barbue's word after so many false alarms, or he'd simply stopped caring about anything or anyone at all.

Minnie, when she sat with him, stroked his face and let her tears roll down her neck to dampen the front of her dress. Initially this, too, seemed to move Ramus. Minnie had seen the worst of everything—she'd seen her own father lynched and hanging from the oak tree in front of her house (the tree she had to pass every time she went to or from school), and her voice didn't even waver when she told the story. She was tough, for sure, but she would be the first to say that she'd told the story too many times to feel it much anymore and also that she absolutely refused to cry about it in front of anyone. But after several days, even Minnie's tears ceased to have an effect on Ramus, and his face remained implacably still. It seemed to Minnie as if she were weeping over a handful of air, or a stone.

She and Barbue were so wound up in their own grief, they kept entirely to themselves, and neither of them had spoken to anyone but Ramus—not even to each other—in nearly a week. When they crossed paths in the trailer they shared, as Barbue was coming home from sitting with Ramus and Minnie was leaving for his trailer, they gave each other the faintest of nods and that was all.

One evening, as Barbue was coming home and Minnie was preparing to leave, they heard the slam of Ramus's trailer door, and both women went running to see who was visiting him or, if it were a miracle, how he'd made it to his feet and wandered outside. From their trailer window, they saw—they both swore to it—a figure that looked to be Tomcat stumble down the trailer steps and out into the night. In his arms, wrapped in a sheet and so frail he might have been a bundle of sticks, was Ramus. His head hung slack against Tomcat's arms; his eyes were closed, and his mouth hung open. Tomcat carried him swiftly toward the river and the line of trees just beyond the midway. Before Minnie or Barbue could shout to stop him, Tomcat had disappeared into the woods, and Ramus was gone.

Ten
The Living Book

WITHOUT RAMUS, THE CAMPFIRE AROUND which everyone took meals was nearly silent. Only a couple handfuls of people were left, and few of them had strong connections with each other. The clown troupe was the exception: they were a strangely insular pack, whispering together and glancing side-eyed at anyone not in their group. Everyone else who was left huddled in pairs: Olympia with Diamond, Madame Barbue with Minnie. Frances, who performed as Blank the Living Book, sat on his own and spoke to no one.

Since they moved into the same trailer, Minnie and Barbue had grown strange and secretive and were rarely seen apart. They left their trailer together in the morning and retired within moments of each other at night. They almost never spoke out loud to anyone anymore, not even to each other; they communicated with each other through long looks and the occasional whisper. They performed their acts mechanically, with neither joy nor even awareness, and abandoned their offstage lives. Both women now wore their costumes always, even while doing chores at the camp. Barbue's yellow dress hung in torn, rotting frills from her hips. The parasol, which she now carried at all times, was irreparably bent; the fabric had pulled away from its wooden ribs, so that it resembled a mangled, bright yellow stork.

They moved and spoke—and thought, it seemed—as one person. "We would like more coffee," Minnie would say to the clown doling it out at the campfire, and both women would hold out their cups in unison. "We are exhausted and need to sleep," Barbue would say, and both women would yawn, walk away and lock themselves inside their shared trailer. When Olympia asked Minnie how she was doing, or asked Barbue if she were feeling all right that morning, one of them (it didn't seem to matter which) would answer, "We're doing just fine, thank you."

Olympia, afraid that she and Diamond would become like Barbue and Minnie now that there were so few people left, made it a point to spend a good part of each day alone. Under the guise of refining her act (which hadn't changed from the first day she'd concocted it, not even the choreography or the flourishes she performed as she sang her song), or of trying to fish in the river (this was, always, an unsuccessful and very damp endeavor that she hated), she would excuse herself from Diamond and wander off on her own.

The good part of the whole ordeal was that, since the night of Tomcat's death, Olympia had been exceedingly solid and hadn't once begun to fade. But the dependable visibility that others took for granted began to feel like a burden. Barbue and Minnie paid her hardly any attention, and there were very few spectators at her shows, but in light of all the disappearances and the rapidly dwindling cast of performers, Diamond had become afraid to let Olympia out of her sight. Although Olympia was glad to have the blinking-out problem gone, there were still many times when she would have liked to fade from view, to be permitted to observe everyone else without having also to be looked at and evaluated. She wanted a bit of rest from being always on some sort of stage, but it only came at night, when Olympia and Diamond were locked in their trailer and Diamond had fallen asleep, or when Olympia was able to get out and away from her and be on her own.

At dawn on the morning after Ramus disappeared, as Olympia prepared her coffee and Diamond followed her silently to and from the trailer and the river and the campfire, she found she'd finally run out of rope.

"Stop it!" She turned on Diamond, who fell back and dropped her tin cup of freshly boiled coffee. It started a brown stain spreading up the line of her dress, but Diamond didn't even seem to notice. Olympia handed over her own mug.

"I was only walking beside you," Diamond said meekly, taking the mug with a small nod of thanks and pressing it to her chest like something precious.

"You were watching over me. You won't stop watching over me."

"I just can't stand it. So many people have disappeared," Diamond said. Then she added, as if it were news to Olympia, "Even Ramus is gone."

"I'm not disappearing, and even if I were, your watching me won't stop it."

"I know," Diamond whispered. She sat on the steps of their trailer, put her head in her hands, and began to cry. Olympia softened and sat beside her.

"I promise; I'm not going to disappear. I haven't even gone invisible in the longest time."

"I know that," Diamond repeated, crying harder.

"Why, then? Why are you crying like this? There's nothing we can do, anyway."

"I'm terrified."

"I'm not going anywhere," Olympia said. "I would feel it if I were in trouble. I don't. I'm not going to disappear."

"I know." Diamond finally looked up, and her eyes were bright with terror. "But what if I do?"

"You won't," Olympia said firmly.

"How can you know that?"

"You just won't."

"Almost everyone else has gone. It could be any one of us next."

"It won't be you; I'm sure of it."

Diamond shook her head. "But you can't know that. I wake up every day and feel for my own arms and legs to make sure I'm still here."

Olympia knew this was true—she'd seen her do it and had taken to doing it herself, once the idea had been presented.

"I won't go, because you so badly need me to stay," Olympia told her. "And you won't go, because I need you, and that will keep you here with me."

Diamond shook her head, smearing at her tears with the back of her hand. She looked incredulous, but she didn't say anything more.

"You'll see," Olympia said.

LATER THAT MORNING, THE GATHERING around the campfire was sober. Nobody spoke in more than grunts and whispers; everyone ate and left as quickly as they could. The silence in the group, interrupted occasionally by the clatter of metal plates and cutlery, was otherwise persistent and oppressive. The clowns, though they'd never cared for Ramus or anyone except themselves, were respectfully quiet, casting frequent furtive glances toward Barbue and Minnie, as if they expected to be screamed at for the slightest move. (It was not a farfetched assumption: one or another of them was often doing something shady or downright dangerous, and they were often screamed at.) Barbue and Minnie huddled whispering over their plates, and no one, not even Olympia, could interrupt them.

Olympia scraped the uneaten food from her plate and dropped the dish in the bin of soapy water for Minnie and Barbue to wash later. She sat down next to Diamond, who was still moving the potatoes and beans around on her plate with a fork.

"You need to finish eating your breakfast," she told her flatly.

"You left yours. I saw you throw almost all of it away," Diamond said.

Olympia didn't respond, but sighed deeply. "I can't stand the silence. I think I might take a walk."

"Don't. The woods will be worse."

From the other side of the campfire, Barbue began to scream. Frances stood, bewildered, as she pointed at his arm and yelled, "Cover it! Cover it!"

On his arm was growing the image of a grave and, beneath that, something like a skull and crossbones made with a diamond ring and two barbells.

* * *

FRANCES HAD GOTTEN HIS FIRST tattoo at age seven, when his sister Mabel had had just about enough of his whining and pigtail grabbing and—in a fit of rage—had stabbed his hand with a fountain pen, leaving a permanent comma-shaped mark on his skin. It was as if, from that day, he'd been indelibly punctuated by that grammatical pause, and Frances became the boy who waited. When others rushed to dive into the swimming hole, he stood on shore and waited to see if any of them encountered something awful in the water; often he waited so long that, by the time he was ready, the sun had set and everyone else had gone home. When every other boy risked love with a local girl who caught his eye, Frances went home alone and waited for his perfect match to come to his door. Of course, she never came. When his friends married and set up households and went to work at the first chance they got, Frances waited to see what opportunities might come his way. He waited so long that eventually anyone he might have married had long been married to someone else and he was left to live alone.

To slow time, instead of settling in a small town and making a family and a name for himself, as most other people he knew had done, he began to cover himself with tattoos; every image, he would say, if asked, represented a memory, a moment of his history he wanted to preserve forever. He had, of course, a rose for his mother (her name had been Rosie). And there was a penny for his father, who'd been a banker. Over his heart, he inked a cartoon heart with the letter C in the center, to remind him of the first girl he ever loved. There was a horseshoe on one thigh to remember the stallion he'd called Commander, the one who was fantastically spirited but had kicked his stall door to smithereens and then run away when Frances was still a young man; and on his other thigh was a clover to remember his grandfather and the lucky streak at cards that had, when it ended, gotten him killed. The art was crude, since he did most of it himself and he was no artist, but it was prolific, and covered nearly every inch of his skin.

When his tattooing extended beyond the collar and cuffs of his shirt to the backs of his hands and his neck, he could no longer find work—was turned away even from a job driving railroad spikes in the hot sun—and gave in to the urge to decorate every piece of skin as yet unmarked, including the empty space of his face. He tattooed a smattering of tears on each cheek, one for each of the great disappointments he'd suffered: his failure in school, his mother's death, the loss of one job after another; after each fresh disappointment, he tattooed another tear, until there was no more room on his cheeks and his face was blue with ink.

When Frances joined the Great Stephens Attraction as the tattooed man (which was, after he'd gone at his own face with ink and needle, one of the only paying opportunities left to him), he discovered that, in the presence of others, his tattoos changed. When he was near a woman whose baby had recently died, an overturned cradle appeared on his shoulder. When a pickpocket brushed against him in a crowd, the image of a rat with its tail caught in a trap rose up on the skin where he had been bumped, and, not more than a few moments later, the thief was caught with his pockets full of watches and wallets. When a local preacher put a hand on him, it left a stain in the shape of a cross dripping blood (and Frances, stricken, tried not to think about what it meant until the reverend was long gone). It was often too difficult to understand the meaning of the images that appeared on his body unless he was given enough information to properly interpret them. A young woman torn between her studies and a proposal of marriage might leave on his body, just from standing nearby, the image of a set of scales, a stack of books, or a fish, and Frances could neither explain nor understand the symbols (though often the person concerned immediately understood and fled from him, pale as a sheet and shaking).

When he began to perform as the tattooed man, he adopted the name Blank the Living Book. He let his tattoos tell the fortunes of those in the crowd. He would allow someone from the audience to come onstage and touch a spot on his body, and then he would ask the person to interpret the image that instantly bubbled up there. Whenever there were too many people near him, when the tent was too full of people pushing toward him on the stage, a riot of new tattoos burst up all at once—a visual cacophony of stories, each overlapping the previous—and his skin boiled with them and stung bitterly. By the end of his brief show, he was always exhausted and in a great deal of pain.

Once they understood what his body did, nobody who knew Frances would touch him or come within a few feet for fear of having their darkest secrets displayed on his flesh. The women he loved would not kiss him or hold him or ever, ever love him back, lest their feelings be inked too clearly on his skin for everyone to see and their virtue thus be called into question. One by one, his friends left him, because not one could bear to see the intimate truth of his life written on Frances's body so clearly. He could not even keep his own thoughts private; the moment he knew something, or felt it, his skin betrayed him and made a picture of it for everyone to see. Neither he nor anyone who came near him could have any secrets, and so Frances spent most of his days alone.

* * *

THOUGH MOST PEOPLE IN THE circus knew not to acknowledge or discuss the images on Frances's skin, the appearance of the grave and the skull and crossbones was unsettling so soon after Ramus's disappearance. The barbells were a clear indication of Ramus, Frances was sure, and Diamond knew her own name when she saw the image manifest itself. What all the images meant together, nobody watching—including Frances himself—was quite sure.

But when Minnie accidentally touched his bicep as she passed to put her plate in the dishwater and a gray raven instantly appeared there like a fingerprint, everyone gasped and whispered. Minnie's hand flew to cover her mouth and she sat down on the ground where she'd stood, not even bothering to move to a log.

"Birds are lost souls," said one of the clowns.

"A raven means death," whispered another.

"No," Minnie said. Her hands shook as she braced herself on the ground and pushed to her feet. She walked swiftly away without a further word.

Barbue stood. "You've done this!" she shrieked at Frances and slapped at his face and arms. Wherever her hand landed, a new, tiny gray bird appeared on his skin. Within moments, he'd gone inky with a swarm of birds and he fell to the ground, writhing in pain as new ones kept appearing.

"Stop!" Olympia shouted and grabbed Barbue's hands. She held them firmly behind Barbue's back until she stopped struggling and went limp. When she was released, Barbue, her voice low and calm, said to Frances, "You've done it to her. You will never be forgiven for it." With that, she turned sharply and marched away, following Minnie to the trailers.

* * *

THE SIDESHOW, WITH THE CONSPICUOUS absence of the World's Strongest Man, became more difficult to maintain. The tattered tent and its poles, along with the equipment it housed, was far too heavy for most of them—even together—to move. So many of the benches had broken that Barbue decided to get rid of them all (they burned them to make the campfires for cooking), and the audience was forced to stand. Minnie, in her grief, had given up on repairing costumes as well as tents, so most of the performers looked like beggars. Their costumes were dirty and ragged and disintegrating even as they wore them. The clowns looked particularly awful.

Olympia worried that if they stayed too long, the police would come looking for Tomcat and the body in the woods would be found. Barbue, Minnie, and Olympia—even Diamond—all seemed to be holding their breaths. They waited and shored themselves up for disaster or rapid flight, but nobody in the town seemed to know or care about Tomcat's disappearance and no police ever came looking for him.

"The best thing for us to do," Diamond told Olympia, "is to stay where we are and change nothing. We can stay hidden in plain sight."

"But everybody looks at us!" Olympia argued. "We make it our profession for everybody to look at us."

"Everybody looks, but nobody sees," Diamond said philosophically.

*   *   *

SOON, NOBODY EVEN LOOKED. OLYMPIA took over barking after Barbue stopped doing it. No matter how enthusiastically Olympia shouted, no matter how enticing she tried to make the wooden signs and the staged lures, the Attraction had stayed too long, and the show itself exuded a depressing air of cheapness, cynicism, and despair. Fewer and fewer people came to the tent, and the few who did come rarely lasted through the whole show.

One day, several weeks after Ramus vanished, it was final: absolutely not a soul came to see them. Barbue forced the entire troupe to wait, not wanting to start the show without an audience, and Blank the Living Book stood onstage at the ready in nothing but a small pair of briefs for over an hour. When the sun had begun to set and still no audience had come, Barbue decided the day was done, and the performers all slogged to their trailers, having done nothing except stand around and having performed for no one at all. Though a couple of the clowns had tried to start a campfire for an evening meal, the fire was paltry and faltering, and not one of the other performers left the trailers to join them.

When, the next afternoon, Frances again stood as Blank on the stage and waited to no avail, and when, again, the sun had set on an empty tent and Barbue had called off the show, Frances decided they would have to move to a new town, as arduous as that would be with such a small crew. He went straight from the stage to speak with Barbue who was, at least erstwhile, the one in charge of such decisions.

"We can't stay here," he told her. "Nobody's coming to see us. We'll die here."

"Impossible to move," she said firmly.

"We can get everyone to help strike the tent—there's only the one— and we don't have that giant water tank anymore, and there are very few trailers, and the horses have been well-rested," he argued.

"Impossible to move now," Barbue said again.

"What are we waiting for?" Frances was frustrated enough to kick the tub of soapy water Barbue had set up for cleaning dishes, though nobody had shown up for the evening meal.

"We must stay here until everyone returns," she said plainly. "Then we can go on."

"Ramus?" Frances cried. "We're waiting for Ramus to come back? He's gone! He's not going to come back!"

Barbue leveled at him such a hard glare that he felt it like a slap.

"Nobody's coming to see us! Not a soul has come for two days! Nobody wants to see us here!"

"Impossible to move now," Barbue repeated and walked off.

* * *

ON THE THIRD DAY WITHOUT an audience, Frances was startled to find that his tattoos had faded to a lighter gray in some places and, in others, had begun to disappear entirely. By that afternoon (which was spent drinking and casting a useless fishing line into the river just to have something to do), only half of the images remained. When

Olympia saw him walking back into the camp at sundown, she cried, "What have you done?"

"Nothing," Frances said. "They're just going on their own."

"Stay out of the sunlight," she told him seriously.

"I don't think it will help," he said. "Half of them disappeared during the night."

Olympia inspected his face: The tattooed tears were completely gone. She inspected his arms and found that the anchor, the umbrella, and the diamond ring were all faded so badly they had become only the faintest traces. The rose and the penny were entirely gone. The eye he'd tattooed on the center of his chest (the one that looked like a crude version of the eye of Ra with beams of light emanating from its pupil) had vanished completely.

"You're fading. You're losing all of them at once."

"I know. I can't stop it."

Olympia wanted to try, and Frances gamely went along with every suggestion. They rubbed oil into his skin and then tried slapping and rubbing it to make his blood flow. She made him eat chicken livers for the next several days, hoping the iron would affect his blood and somehow stop the ink from wearing away. Nothing seemed to have an effect. If anything, with every passing day, the tattoos seemed to be disappearing faster.

Olympia took him to consult with some of the clowns, who all hid tattoos of their own under their costumes and makeup, but not a one could offer a suggestion about what was happening, or why, or how to stop it.

By the sixth day, when Frances woke, the images had eroded so completely that his skin was almost entirely empty. As terrified as he was, he felt lighter, too, as if each disappeared drawing had released him from a burden. But what remained—his unadorned, pale skin—seemed monstrous. He looked to himself like a grub that spent its entire life in the dark of the soil; he was unstained as an empty teacup, blank as a sheet of paper, unwritten upon, and ugly. By the seventh day, every last mark on his body was gone and, by the eighth, his skin had continued to fade so drastically that it was nearly transparent, and one could see his heart squeezing like a fist, could see the blood run blue and red through the twists of vein, could see the organs and muscles and bones, as if both inside and outside were the same. He repulsed even himself, bundled up until the least amount of his body was visible, and stayed in his trailer. By the ninth day, his skin had nearly disappeared entirely, as had the color from his hair and eyes, and his organs had begun to wane into colorlessness and translucence. By the tenth day, he had completely disappeared.

Eleven
General Error and the Mistakes of Nature

Though she—and everyone else in the Attraction—missed him, Olympia felt it like a weight off her back when Frances was gone. Those who remained—Barbue, Minnie, the clowns—kept to themselves and all but ignored Olympia and Diamond. They could walk together without fear and did not worry that a touch in public was too lingering or a look too full of meaning. Though Diamond didn't seem to notice or change her behavior much, Olympia felt it in her body: Her muscles stayed loose, and she could, finally, draw a full lungful of air when she breathed just knowing that if her hand happened to brush Diamond's cheek when they walked outside, if she happened to smile too broadly at her or laugh with her in too familiar a way, no harm would come of it.

Once, when the two were kneeling together over a tub of soapy river water and scrubbing clean a basin of clothes, Olympia's heart squeezed hard when Diamond sat back and wiped a sweaty arm across her cheek, leaving it streaked with dirt. Olympia did not hesitate to wipe gently at the smear and push Diamond's hair back from her face and she was, without a second's thought, able to say, "I love you." The sun was a warm hand on her neck and a pollen-heavy breeze ruffled the short hair on the back of her head; everything smelled of the soap they were using to wash the clothes: sharp and clean. It was a fragrant, golden moment, and so strange to say those words outside, in the sunlight and air, not hidden in the dark of the mildewing trailer. She quickly kissed the tip of Diamond's nose. Despite all the disappearances and the dwindling supply of food and money, she felt, perhaps truly for the first time in her life, safe and solid and real.

Olympia found every excuse, after that, to keep Diamond outside for the rest of the day. They walked to the river to fetch water and to try fishing again; this time, between the two of them, they managed to catch three fish, so they would have food for the next several days. They fed and watered and brushed the Attraction's few remaining horses.

That night, when they were tired and curled up together in bed, the trailer did not seem so oppressive.

Still, though Diamond hadn't mentioned it again, Olympia could not forget her question: "What if I disappear?" She clutched the sleeping woman in her arms, buried her nose in the honey smell of her hair, and did not fall asleep for a long time.

* * *

OLYMPIA AND DIAMOND WERE JUST returning from a trip to the neighboring farm, their pockets full of eggs bought with their few remaining pennies, when Minnie, looking wild with terror, pulled them into her trailer.

"Police!" she hissed, indicating that they should make absolutely no noise.

"What should we do?" Diamond whispered back.

"Stay here and stay down. I'm going to go out there and find Barbue and make sure everything is okay."

"But they'll see you." Olympia wrapped her hands in the hem of Minnie's dress and held on. "They're probably looking for you, and Barbue, too!"

"I'll find Madame Barbue," Diamond volunteered. She started to stand, but Minnie grabbed her arm, pulled her back to the ground, and whispered a desperate, "No!" She stood instead, and took a moment to right her dress and hair before confidently striding out and down the trailer steps to the midway. Olympia and Diamond hid against the wall beneath the window, both too scared to crane their necks up and look out to see, perhaps, a glimpse of Barbue or the police or the goings-on outside. They huddled together and clutched hands. In the stillness and safety of the trailer, Olympia began to calm—until she heard Diamond's rapid breathing.

"Don't," she said. "It will all be all right."

"If they take me—"

"They won't," Olympia soothed. "This can't be about Tomcat. They would have come sooner. And nobody here will blame you for that. It was Ramus who killed him, and Ramus is gone." It hurt her to say it, but the effect on Diamond was worth it; she began to breathe more quietly and her grip on Olympia's hand loosened slightly.

"If they find me, they're going to take me because I am his wife."

"They won't find you," Olympia said. "Nobody here is going to tell them where you are. Even the clowns know better than to do that. We'll all protect you."

Diamond said nothing. Though her hand had relaxed its hold and was no longer crushing Olympia's, her breath continued its uneven hitching, and she began to sob quietly. Olympia kissed the top of her head and held her tightly until the door burst open and Minnie came in.

"It's not about Tomcat," Minnie said, breathless. "It's not about Tom. Everything is fine. I couldn't find Barbue, but the police don't want her anyway. And," she added, warmly cupping Diamond's cheek, "they don't want you, either, sweetheart. They don't want any of us."

"My god," Olympia breathed. "My god. I knew it; I did, but thanks for that, anyway."

Minnie knelt down next to Diamond and shook her shoulder gently.

"Do you hear me, Diamond? They are not coming for any of us. They aren't here about Tomcat. Everything is fine."

Something inside Diamond seemed to crumble, and she went limp against Olympia's side and burst into tears. Olympia pulled her closer, locked her arm around Diamond's shoulder, and tried to make herself feel as imposing and steady as she could. It was not much, but it was the best she could do.

"That's right," Minnie cooed at Diamond. "Everything is fine. The police aren't here about Tomcat."

Minnie's words were soothing, but they made Olympia's blood stop running. If the police weren't investigating Tomcat, then they'd come to the circus on some other business, and that could not turn out well for any of them. "But then," Olympia dared, "if they aren't here about Tomcat, why are they here?"

"They're here about pickpockets," Minnie said.

"We don't have pickpockets!" Olympia said. "We don't even have an audience! No pockets to pick!"

Minnie looked straight at Olympia in surprise.

"They're arresting the clowns."

* * *

WHEN GENERAL ERROR WAS A young man, he was called Darwin. Before that, he was named Charles. Both his mother and father were teachers—his mother at a small schoolhouse, his father at the Atlanta College of Physicians and Surgeons. Hoping he would follow his father into medical study and wanting him to have a name that sounded as important as they knew he would someday be, his parents called him Darwin. He was introduced to guests and new friends in this way and, when they enrolled him in school, they wrote the name "Darwin" on the register. Though they'd named him Charles, they never once called him anything but Darwin.

Much to his parents' disappointment, Darwin was a terrible student, and especially excelled at failing in every scientific and mathematical subject he studied. He left school before he turned fifteen and, at sixteen, he left home for good to try his hand at acting. He was good-looking enough to be given parts in several plays, but soon earned a reputation as an idiot who could neither emote convincingly nor remember his lines; the plays in which he acted were resounding flops, and the failures were mostly—if not entirely—due to Darwin's contributions. Still, he refused to work in a factory or, worse, as a shopkeeper, or at any other mundane job in which, being an artist at heart, he knew he did not want to compromise himself. What he lacked in talent he made up for in confidence and perseverance. He painted his face and began to practice pantomime, an art for which his inflated expressions and scenery-chewing sense of drama were perfectly suited. He worked where he could, sometimes in a theatrical production and sometimes on a street corner with a cup set out for spare change.

When, years later, the traveling Attraction came to town, it was as if Fate had stepped in and handed him the most wonderful idea Charles-cum-Darwin had ever had.

He made his plea directly to Magnus, and his offer to bring a troupe of comedy pantomime performers (starring, of course, himself) to the Attraction's stage was immediately accepted. Darwin found his troupe in a tavern, so inebriated they could barely rouse enough balance and wit to stand up and follow him into the street. They were a handful of drunks and lost souls and halfwits, but it took little convincing to gain their allegiance. Darwin organized them into several routines, and, with practice and the promise of pay enough to live on, they were able to coordinate an excellent, funny, and wordless performance.

Being mostly unattached and unsuccessful, the troupe of men easily left their homes and followed Darwin to The Stephens Great Attraction, where they ate together and slept together like a pile of dogs in one large trailer. They honed their act in the mornings and performed in the afternoons. The evenings were reserved for drinking and banter and the general harassment of any women they could locate for their purposes (this was not often achieved). Before long, however, they discovered the weakness of their paychecks: Food was scarce and liquor was almost entirely out of reach.

They were a bunch of grifters—several smug misanthropes, one man who was dying too slowly for his family to afford, two boys who had run away from their homes, a man who had lost his farm and was desperate to send money home to his starving family—who had spent most of their days tanked and most of their nights alone. When they formed The Mistakes of Nature to provide backup antics for Darwin's stage clown General Error, they made a family (or, perhaps more accurately, they formed an organization). They rigged a system for grift, two clowns each day taking responsibility for the day's work picking the pockets of the Attraction spectators. The stolen goods were hocked for cash in the next town; the profits of the pawn were then shared amongst them all, no matter who had done the stealing. They grew into a tightly knit band of thieves, more concerned with getting a good take on any given day than with putting on a good performance, though they limited themselves to picking pockets only once in every town, in case word spread and the pockets came to the circus prophylactically emptied. Darwin felt the reins slipping out of his hands as more new and uninitiated performers—invited by one or another of the current clowns—showed up every week. The new ones were rarely skilled comedians and were chosen for their ability as thieves or their general seediness and willingness to do anything for money. Over and over again, Darwin told his clowns that the organization could brook no more members, but the clowns didn't listen, and their numbers kept increasing until there were at least twelve, perhaps fourteen of them, and only a few who were sober and fit enough to perform without making children cry.

Though the troupe had seemed to take on a life of its own, growing bigger and more unwieldy than Darwin could control, he stayed with them, afraid to lose the only success and family he'd known in his life. If he walked away, Darwin had nowhere to go, and nobody else on whom he could depend. So he stayed with The Mistakes of Nature, kept his mouth shut, and watched as the troupe grew larger and more dangerously insular every week. Soon, they associated only with their own, eschewing at all times the company of the other circus performers, most especially those in the sideshow. Darwin himself was not bothered by the strangeness of the bearded lady or the world's tiniest man, but his clowns often muttered, "Freaks!" and, mustering their darkest looks, scuttled away before contact with any of them had to be made. They trusted only each other, and barely that—it was only the code of honor among thieves that kept them as organized as they were. Once Magnus disappeared, they stopped limiting their criminal work and took to pocket-picking at every performance, no matter the danger. Though Darwin argued against this practice, he was sorely outnumbered and no longer in control. But with the disappearance of their audiences went the pockets for picking, and the band had to resort to other methods (stealing fruit and chickens from nearby farms, hustling cards in the local tavern) just to get by. They grew, as a bunch, gaunt and foul-tempered, and they began to scheme how to get enough money to buy a good supper.

When the police showed up, it was no surprise to Darwin, and several of the other clowns looked resigned—even relieved—to see them. Though the clowns tried to use their numbers and their anonymity to hornswoggle the cops out of finding the ones they wanted to arrest, eventually four of the clowns were taken away in handcuffs and the take from an entire day as evidence.

The clowns who remained were hardly surprised—let alone saddened—by the capture of their cohort; most of them were more dismayed by the loss of their loot, and they weren't deterred in the slightest from returning to business as usual. Within an hour of the police's departure with their friends, the remaining clowns made a plan for a performance that would allow them to work with fewer numbers and still increase their take of stolen goods. Two of them (their names mattered little, even to each other, but the clowns in questions were a tall one who wore a pointed, spotted dunce cap and a very short one in a bright red wig) were dispatched to town to drum up a crowd who would follow them back to the show as if they were pied but pipeless pipers.

Though the two men stood outside the general store for hours, putting on a free show of pratfalls and hyperbolized mishaps, and though they managed to draw a small crowd of spectators, they were unsuccessful in bringing many back to the circus and only managed to lure in a paltry audience of four people.

Still, an audience of four was four bigger than they'd had in days, and everyone was eager to perform again. Diamond pulled on her glass-studded outfit, and Olympia climbed into her half-dress to become Nova. They waited at the side of the stage with Barbue and Minnie, watching General Error and a slightly reduced collection of Mistakes run circles around each other onstage as the stoic audience of four sat still as statues, as if determined to remain unamused no matter what the clowns did. At the climax of their act, all the clowns piled into a hollowed-out American Underslung with red curtains hung all around the doors and windows, and General Error drove them off the stage.

This was, at least, how it usually happened. On this occasion, they all piled in—more clowns than should fit in the vehicle, though fewer than were usually crammed into it—and pulled the curtains closed so the audience couldn't see how they'd packed themselves in. Darwin got in last, and the car puttered forward as it was meant to do. After a few feet, however, it rolled to a stop and stayed there for far too long. After a few moments of grumbling from the handful of people watching, when it looked as if they were all about to leave, Minnie rushed forward and pulled back the red curtains. The car was empty.

The audience broke into cheers of surprise and delight, clapping and—in the case of one toothless graybeard who seemed particularly enthusiastic—even standing. Minnie was bewildered, and looked as if she was, which seemed to the outsiders like great showmanship. Olympia's chest clutched her heart tightly; she knew it already, before anyone confirmed it: the clowns had disappeared like the others.

* * *

It was, though neither Olympia nor anyone else would admit it, a relief to be rid of the clowns, who'd grown bitter and mean and secretive. A clown who would only answer to Toto (Olympia was sure his name was Tony, but he wouldn't acknowledge anyone who called him that) had been persistently awful to Olympia and Diamond; it seemed as though he'd sniffed out their secret togetherness, or perhaps seen them in an unguarded moment, and was bent on turning their desire in his direction, or punishing them, or perhaps both. Every time he got near Diamond or Olympia, he whispered the crudest, most violent fantasies into their ears, and yet he managed to look happy and innocent as soon as he was in front of an audience. A handful of the other men had been menacing Minnie, calling her a dirty Creole and a fat sow, refusing to eat anything she'd helped to prepare or serve, and whistling while happily twirling what was meant to look like a hanging rope. Barbue they tolerated (perhaps the beard gave her some credibility in their eyes, or perhaps they were rightfully scared of her), though they neither trusted nor liked her and made that clear at every opportunity. The clowns who hadn't actively bothered anyone had watched it happen and said nothing. Even Darwin had remained passively silent, well aware that he had lost all power over the lot long ago, and not caring enough to stick his neck out in any case.

The disappearance of the clowns was an immense relief to everyone who remained at the circus. At the earliest opportunity after they'd gone, Barbue and Minnie pushed the clowns' American Underslung into the river and let it bubble down to the bottom.

When the clowns and the police were both gone, when the sun had set and the clowns' car had sunk to the river bottom, Barbue declared that they were stuck for good and took the few remaining horses into town and sold them. With the little money that brought (it was not much—the horses were stringy-legged and mane-matted and in very poor shape), she bought a handful of vegetables, some soap, some buckshot, and some salt—that, and any fish they managed to catch or birds they managed to shoot, would have to suffice for the foreseeable future. The four of them ate a paltry meal at the campfire, silent except for Minnie's weeping and Barbue's attempts to comfort her, then retired to their trailers for the night, and Olympia and Diamond breathed in the peace, finally, of their privacy.

With every departure from the circus Olympia and Diamond felt a little less hindered, a little less frightened of being discovered. This was true even of the disappearances of those they missed, like Ramus or Arnold. Neither woman was able to relax, however, because even though the disappearances meant they were less likely to be discovered, every disappearance also left them more alone, and they were *unexplained* disappearances and frightening for that reason alone.

Diamond kept a bag of clothes packed and hidden under the cot, though she thought Olympia didn't know about it. Olympia kept her eye on Diamond at all times, worried she'd leave without even a goodbye if the situation got too frightening or dire. Each night, she secretly removed one item from Diamond's packed case—she knew it would probably do no good, but it gave her a sense of peace.

On the fourth morning after the clowns had disappeared, Olympia blocked the trailer door before Diamond could leave for the day.

"Are you going away?" she asked.

Diamond stopped and looked at her carefully—her face at first a picture of bewilderment and then, once Olympia's eyes shifted to indicate the case under the cot, dawning fear.

"I wasn't going to go, not really, and definitely not without saying goodbye to you."

"Where?"

"To find my daughter," Diamond said.

"We've talked about this. You can't do that."

"I wouldn't take her away with me. I just want to see her and know she's okay."

"Diamond," Olympia pleaded. "That's too dangerous. Please. You can't."

"I have to know," she said. "I have to just see her with my own eyes, or it's like she's gone forever."

"She is."

"What?"

"Gone forever," Olympia said. "She is."

"I—" Diamond began.

"People disappear forever," Olympia said simply. "People you love, even. Even though you did nothing wrong, you're going to lose people. You're going to lose everyone in your life, if you live long enough."

"Not my daughter."

"Even her."

Diamond was quiet, but she shook her head violently, biting her lip.

"You're going to lose me one day, or I'm going to lose you," Olympia told her. "Don't go now and disappear. It's bad enough around here, without you going, too."

"But if we stay here, we'll both end up gone."

"We won't. We'll figure out how to stay with each other. Even if we disappear, we can disappear together," Olympia said. "The clowns did, and I'm sure wherever they've got to, they're all in the same place."

"I don't think they're in any place at all. What if they just stopped *being* anywhere? What if they're not gone *to* somewhere, what if they're just *gone*?"

Olympia had no answer. She'd never felt so small, or so frightened, in her life. She knew she was flickering, half-visible, but Diamond said nothing about it. She burst into tears, buried her face against Diamond's shoulder, and cried until she was exhausted. The last thing she remembered of that evening was Diamond slowly pulling off her clothes, putting her into a fresh nightgown, and putting her to bed before climbing into the cot next to her and holding her tightly around the waist.

"I won't go," she whispered to Olympia. "I promise I won't go."

Twelve
The Princess of Largesse

THE NEXT MORNING, BARBUE BANGED on their trailer door not long after the sun had risen. Olympia, exhausted from weeping herself to sleep, could barely tear herself out of the cot to let Barbue inside.

"She's gone, Minnie's gone," Barbue could barely wheeze out. "I woke this morning and she was gone, but her bags and all of her clothes and shoes are still in the trailer!"

"She's probably gone to the river for water," Olympia said.

"No! No, I checked the river before I came to you! And all of her clothes and shoes are still there," Barbue wailed.

Diamond sat up and pushed the hair out of her eyes. "What? Are you all right, Madame?" she asked.

"Minnie's gone!" Barbue made no effort, now that Diamond was awake, to control her volume and she burst into noisy tears.

Diamond immediately pushed herself out of bed and, without dressing, ran out the door and into the trailer Minnie and Barbue shared. Madame Barbue and Olympia followed, but by the time they'd gotten in behind her, Diamond was already digging in Minnie's cupboard.

"Her bags are still here, and her shoes, and all her dresses," Diamond said.

"It's what I said!" Barbue's tears began afresh.

Diamond began to dig under the cot, pulling out a pair of slippers, an extra blanket, and a steamer trunk.

"What's this?" she asked. "It's as heavy as a boulder."

"I don't know," Barbue said. She dropped to the floor and pulled the lid open. Olympia fell down beside her, and the three of them looked through the trunk together.

Inside was a large and strange collection of items; among the piles of junk were a handful of hairpins, quite a large number of stones and good-sized rocks, several balls of wadded paper, two Bibles, some crumpled paper cups, a rolled-up newspaper, five dried-out apples and a paper-wrapped sandwich. There was nothing else in the trunk, although its bottom was sandy with handfuls of loose dirt.

"I don't understand," Diamond said. "Why would she keep these things? There are no letters, no mementos, or anything worth saving in here, except the books." She batted aside a few of the paper cups in irritation.

"They threw those," Barbue said.

"The books?" Diamond asked.

"At the stage. The audience. When Minnie was onstage. Sometimes they even threw rocks," Olympia said. "And the hairpins. I saw them throw those, too."

"All of it," Madame Barbue said, her voice thick. "Every single thing in this trunk."

Diamond shuddered. "Why would anyone keep this?"

"I never saw her do it," Barbue said. "But Minnie must have collected it after every show."

* * *

SHE WAS BORN AMELIA CELESTE LePont, fat and poor, the middle daughter of three born to Modeste and Emile LePont. They lived in a last-resort neighborhood on the outskirts of New Orleans, a cobbled-together parish of shacks and swaying little houses owned by Black Creole folks, all of them too poor to choose a better place to live (and in this case it was exactly as they said about beggars not being able to be choosers). When she was born, her mother used to say proudly, she was such a fat little baby the doctor almost had to cut Modeste open to get Amelia out. When Amelia was a girl, everyone envied Modeste and Emile—the other Creole children were sallow, gaunt, and furious with hunger, but Amelia was fat, bright, and unflaggingly happy. Her own sisters were thin as rails, though they were fed no differently than Amelia. She was much paler than her sisters or either of her parents, and, when they went into town to shop, strangers always mistook her for a lost little white girl, even when she was with her family, and tried to rescue her away from them.

Her family called her Minnie because, as Emile said jokingly, she was no small problem.

When she had barely reached nine years old, her father was hung by the neck from rope strung in the oak tree near their front door; her mother, her two sisters, and Minnie all watched from the corner of a window as her father was dragged screaming from the cowshed by several hooded men, fitted with a noose, and hoisted into the arms of the tree. The men stood there watching until her father had ceased to move and he was surely dead; his children could do nothing but hide and witness it. It turned her stomach, even decades later, to remember the broken way her father's body jerked in the air and then suddenly stopped moving entirely, and the way her mother's hand held her arm so tightly to keep her from yelling or running to save him that her nails cut half-moons of blood into Minnie's skin. Minnie and her sisters had struggled so hard against her, had so hysterically cried, that Modeste locked them in a closet until the men had gone and she had cut Emile's body down from the tree, dragged it as far as she could into the tall reeds near the swamp, and buried it under a layer of mud and Spanish moss where her daughters wouldn't see it.

From that night on, Modeste kept all three girls in the house. She refused to go out to the market, the garden, or even the cowshed in the daylight, and wouldn't let any of the girls out for play or school. Their neighbor, a watchful older woman called Virginie, brought them a basket of food every few days (the simplest of gifts, what she could spare to help: turnips and collards with a bit of bread and a few pats of butter), but there was little they could do with the vegetables since Modeste, afraid the smoking chimney would draw attention and bring the hanging men back for them, refused to light the stove.

Minnie spent the long hours between waking and going to bed huddled behind the stove with her sisters Isabelle and Perrine. Since they were not allowed to go to school, Isabelle, who was the oldest by one year, gave them lessons from her father's books and read them stories when they grew bored with spelling exercises. At midnight, when there was not even moonlight by which they could see, their mother would wake them and let them play in the cowshed, though they were forbidden to scream or laugh or even speak to each other above a whisper and there was barely room for the three of them to walk in a circle, let alone run. They ate once, in the evenings, tiny portions of turnips or apples or, when they were very lucky, bread; sometimes their mother would allot them a small amount of raw collards on which to chew in the mornings as well.

"Hard times," her mother had called it. Amelia and her sisters took the phrase on: When they were hungry, when they were sad, or tired, or wanted desperately to play in the sun, they'd shake their heads, looking grim, and mutter, "Hard times," and the others would nod seriously, as if everything that needed to be said had been said, and they all understood, though not a one of them did.

It soon became apparent to the three girls that their mother was not well. She spent most of the day at the front window, staring out past the tree and into the distance, poised for any hint of something coming down the road, neglecting food and rest and, sometimes, forgetting to breathe. More than once, Amelia or one of her sisters came upon their mother flopped in a dead faint against the windowsill and had to revive her with shouts and shaking and tears. Even so, Modeste seemed not to remember for long stretches of the day that her daughters were there with her, or that they needed to eat or be put to bed or cared for beyond fierce protection against the hangmen.

One afternoon, while the three girls studied behind the woodstove, Modeste walked out of the house, past the tree where her husband had been killed, and kept walking up the road until she was nothing but a tiny speck on the horizon, and then kept walking until she was gone.

In their mother's absence, Isabelle instituted the same system of rules as Modeste had done: a little food for breakfast, more at dinner, no going outside except for silent midnight exercise in the cow shed. This went on for several days, until Virginie came to deliver a basket of collards and found the three girls, dirty and wide-eyed, crouching behind the stove; Modeste, they told her, was long gone. Virginie took the girls to her own home, fed them, washed their clothes and made them bathe (they had not bathed in weeks and they smelled terrible, though they'd stopped smelling their own stink); she tucked them into her own bed and slept curled at the foot where their legs didn't reach. They stayed with her, and Isabelle and Perrine grew thick and rosy again; Minnie remained the same as she ever was, soft, wide, too large to fit comfortably in the spaces she was given, but her skin grew warmer-toned and sanguine, and, when Virginie taught her to make biscuits or showed her how to count the household money into careful piles, her eyes glittered and she looked, despite everything, like a normal, happy child.

Within a year, Isabelle left to make a home with a young man called Amé, who took her to Vermilion to start a farm. Perrine and Minnie began to work together in the kitchen of one of New Orleans' oldest white Creole families, shucking corn and shelling peas until their fingers were raw and swollen. Perrine hated the work passionately, hated Miss Amandine, who ran the kitchen, even more, and within weeks had packed her bags and fled in the middle of the night for anywhere else.

Minnie lived with Virginie and cooked in the Patins' kitchen for four years. Virginie was loving and stern, the smartest teacher she'd ever had, and a very good mother. When Minnie, on a rare trip into

New Orleans to buy cloth and a new hammered iron pot (the bottom had burned clean out of the old one), met Madame Barbue, who was also inquiring after a new pot, they became instant friends. Barbue spoke very odd French, more nasal and drawn out than the American southern patois Minnie was used to hearing, and she was the oddest combination of rough and soft: wiry hair and cottony pale skin stretched over sharp, hard muscles and bones. The skin of her forearms was dusted with thick brown hair, and when she smiled, she revealed a large gap left by three missing front teeth. Minnie had never seen a woman like Barbue, and when Barbue invited her to visit the sideshow the next afternoon, Minnie went secretly and by herself, sensing that the show was salacious enough that she shouldn't tell Virginie where she was going and knowing she would not go home again.

It turned out that she did return home, in order to gather her things and properly thank Virginie for all she'd done to help Minnie and her long-gone sisters, but within days she joined Barbue in her trailer at the Attraction. The two of them almost never spoke English, but preferred a rapid, twisting French that bent itself between Minnie's rolling patois and Barbue's nasal and self-consciously precise Québécois. Barbue coached Minnie to become the Fat Lady in the sideshow. This took far more than Minnie's ampleness; she adopted a character to suit the role (queenly, haughty, greedy), and developed a costume and routine designed to best allow people to appreciate her strangeness (this involved, in large part, eating cake, the sight of which soon made her sick to her stomach, and patting her cheeks with face powder until she appeared white as a ghost). Through performing, she learned to absorb the audience's moods—anger and disappointment, fear and hunger and want—with resigned placidity. When, during the course of the show, the audience grew rowdy, shouting insults and throwing their garbage in her direction, she sat and smiled and ate her cake until her show ended. Then she quietly scooped up the detritus that had landed at her feet, slipped backstage and made her way to the anonymity and stillness of her trailer.

After just a few weeks of performing, she had made quite a collection of the objects hurled at her while she was onstage and dedicated a trunk under her bed for keeping it. Every few weeks the trunk grew so full of rocks and paper and other projectiles that she had to empty it; wherever the Attraction set up camp, she'd sneak out in the dead of night to dig a hole and bury the trunk's contents, only to start her collection again the next day. Within another few weeks, she'd empty the trunk and start all over. It wasn't as if she wanted to keep the mementos; it was more that she couldn't bear to throw them away, as if to do so would be to turn her head from the misery she knew was often behind the desire to throw things at her. In her wake, she planted, as the circus traveled from poor town to poorer town to backwoods swampland, the seeds of misery.

* * *

AFTER MINNIE'S DISAPPEARANCE, IT WAS just the three of them. Barbue kept mostly to herself, coming out of her trailer only to bathe and to light the fire for cooking twice a day. Olympia made her own fire for cooking, and she and Diamond saw Barbue only when their paths crossed coincidentally on the way to or from the river. Without Minnie, Barbue had lapsed into a mournful silence; her face was drawn and haggard, her beard matted, and she communicated, when they passed, only through nods and soft grunts.

Olympia and Diamond spent most of their days knee-deep in the stream washing clothes or trying to catch fish to feed the three of them. They made a pittance on good days, when the two went into town and performed on a street corner (Olympia as the half-man balancing on a large ball, and Diamond swallowing a sword), but after they shared their day's take with Barbue, there was hardly enough left to buy a small amount of flour or a half-dozen eggs on which they might sustain themselves for a little while longer.

For her part, Barbue was useless for performing or doing anything that involved interacting with other people, but she did her best to keep the camp clean and mend what needed to be mended. She cooked every meal, and was miraculously skilled at turning a paltry handful of ingredients into good and satisfying food. She stopped crying at every turn, and steeled herself into a determined stoicism that impressed Olympia; once Barbue was resolved, she was hard to crack. Diamond helped when she could, but had few skills, aside from some basic knowledge of cleaning and cooking; she had to be shown how to scale and bone a fish, had to be shown how to husk corn and devein collards. What she lacked in skill she made up for in patience and resolve, however, and she quickly became Barbue's favorite as an apprentice.

Olympia happily gutted and skinned the fish for Diamond while she listened to Barbue prattle on in her nasal French, sometimes a song, and sometimes a long, chanting recital—she assumed Barbue was telling stories of her youth, or reciting poems from school, or perhaps imparting tips and instructions for proper cooking. The tone, if not the content, of her words was clear; the meaning would, Olympia assumed, be forever a mystery. When she spoke, when she chanted in her singsong voice, the birds stopped chattering and the crickets went silent; it seemed as if the entire meadow was listening to Barbue, though Olympia doubted the birds understood Barbue any better than she or Diamond did. Barbue might have been reciting a list of chores, or of words she thought were funny-sounding, for all anyone—birds most likely included—could tell. But it was rhythmic and hypnotic; Barbue rocked and worked to a beat when she spoke or sang like this, and it was, for all of them, immensely comforting.

Gradually, Olympia began to notice that Diamond walked with an odd, loping gait and that she would cling to the nearest fence post or tree or door handle when she wasn't moving, as if to steady herself. After a few days, she had taken to walking, clumsily and slowly, only with the aid of a long stick, which she dug into the ground with every step and used to propel herself forward as if it were a skiff pole. Upon more careful inspection, Olympia discovered that Diamond's feet were no longer quite touching the ground, as if she were floating a half-inch above the dust at all times.

"You're floating now," Olympia said, as if the fact were mundane and not, as it was, a matter of great concern.

"I haven't been able to touch the ground for days," Diamond admitted, shaking her head. She clung, as she spoke, to the door of the trailer. "I'm starting to be afraid that a strong wind will carry me off."

They decided not to tell Barbue, who would likely panic and worry more than was useful, but from that moment, Olympia watched Diamond carefully. She dug under Minnie's cot and pulled out the trunk full of hurled debris, and she filled Diamond's pockets with the rocks so that she would always be weighted down enough to touch the ground. This worked for a time, though with every hour, she had to add another rock to each pocket to keep Diamond grounded. By that afternoon, when the two went to the river to fish, Diamond's pockets were overflowing with rocks and still her toes barely brushed the road.

It was a temporary solution to a problem neither of them could solve. When, forgetting herself for a moment, Diamond took off her dress and dived into the river to bathe (she had not done so for a week, and the dirt was beginning to sting in the creases of her skin), she realized too late that the rocks that were keeping her steady were in the pockets of the dress she'd just discarded. She began to float rapidly skyward, her white undergarments dripping with river water as she went. She shouted for Olympia, who came running and managed to knock Diamond sideways under the cover of a large tree before she floated, unhindered, clear up into the sky and disappeared. As it was, she was snared in the tree in her sopping underclothes and managed, with the consequence of not a few scratches, to climb through the branches and back down to Earth, where she clung to the tree trunk and cried, panting and soaked and shivering.

Olympia tied a rope around her own waist, then looped it around Diamond's with a little slack between, so that she was tethered to her more solid, grounded body and could not float away again. They had to explain to Barbue, who, as predicted, panicked and fussed and worried herself to bed that night, not knowing what more could be done to keep Diamond from floating off. It wasn't practical, Barbue insisted, to tie Diamond to Olympia in that way, and she worried what would happen if the rope broke. Olympia assured her that would not happen, but Diamond agreed to wear anklets of stones to keep her grounded.

The stones, however, rubbed her skin raw, and had to be discarded only hours after they'd been affixed. The tether, Olympia assured Barbue, would suffice—it would have to. From that moment, they spent every second tied to one another, Diamond floating behind and just above Olympia's shoulder as she walked. At night, as they slept, Olympia lay on top of Diamond to keep her in the bed; otherwise, she hovered a few feet above it and wept in desperation like a mournful spirit, and neither of them could get any rest.

Thirteen
The Bearded Lady

WHEN THE SUN ROSE, OLYMPIA lit a campfire and set a pot of water to boil while Diamond floated above her like a hot air balloon. They waited there for more than an hour, but Madame Barbue did not appear. With a sinking feeling, Olympia went to Barbue's trailer and banged on the door, but there was no answer.

"She's gone," Diamond wailed from somewhere just above Olympia's shoulder. "She's left us alone!"

Olympia grunted and pushed the door open with a heavy shove. The trailer was so pristine it appeared empty: No clothing hung in the closet, no teacup sat on the counter, not a handkerchief could be found anywhere in the little room, and Minnie's trunk was gone from under the bed. Olympia assumed that all of Barbue's things were stored neatly away somewhere else, though she could not figure where they'd been put. The floor and the tabletops shone as if they'd been buffed moments before. Other than a cheery spray of wildflowers in a vase on the table and the scissors and handheld mirror Barbue used to trim her beard placed precisely next to the vase, there was not a single personal touch nor sign of life in the whole place; it was as if Madame Barbue had never existed. Or, Olympia thought it more likely, Barbue had packed up her things and struck out on her own in the middle of the night. On further thought, however, Olympia wasn't quite so sure it wasn't something worse, because Barbue wouldn't have left without telling them, and, in any case, she wasn't strong enough to haul a trunk of her own clothing by herself and had sold the horses off. She rummaged through the neatly made beds and the empty closets for any clue as to what might have happened to Barbue while Diamond hovered above her and sobbed. When she pulled open Minnie's pillow, a fat envelope fell out, spilling a load of coins onto the bedsheet.

"Barbue didn't take this, at least." Olympia ran her hand across the money. "She must not have known."

"How much is it?" Diamond asked.

"Looks like over fifteen dollars. That'll last us for a bit, if we just buy vegetables."

Olympia gathered the coins back into the envelope while Diamond sobbed quietly from her place near the trailer's ceiling. The envelope, both beds, the softening overstuffed chair, even the coins—everything smelled somehow of Barbue's perfume, like dense and cloying orange flower water.

* * *

THE DAY CHRISTMAS LEVESQUE TURNED sixteen was the last day of her childhood and the first day of a life that would be—her mother told her—riddled with hardship. She'd been working long before then, of course, helping her father to skin the animals he trapped and tan the hides and helping her mother to tend house, cook, and raise the crops, but it was becoming clear that the little wisps of hair that had begun to sprout along her jaw were not going away, were only getting thicker, darker, and wirier. Behind her back (though she and everyone else could easily hear the whispers), the women in the neighborhood called her *La Fille Barbue*—The Bearded Girl.

Christmas was stringy and coarse-mannered and by all estimations far too manly for a young woman, and not a single suitor had once looked her way. Her parents knew—and Christmas knew—that this would only get worse as she grew taller, as the beard on her chin refused to fade, as her skin grew leatherier with sun and her arms grew thicker with muscle. Her mother stopped giving her lessons in needlework (which was for the best, since her hands were too meaty and clumsy to make anything of beauty), and stopped asking her to help with the cooking of meals (which was also for the best, since Christmas had hopelessly inaccurate taste and an impatience in the kitchen which caused her to mangle, burn, or otherwise ruin everything she touched). Her father stopped speaking of suitors ("You must learn how to skin a rabbit," he used to say, "because someday your husband will ask it of you,") and began, instead, to prepare her for a life alone. ("You must learn to butcher a rabbit," he began to tell her, "or you will starve.")

On her sixteenth birthday, Christmas was allowed to accompany her father and his friends into the woods to empty and reset the fur traps. The small group of them—Christmas, her father Henri, his friends M. Janvier and M. Moreau, and a friend of M. Janvier's, an awful, pockmarked younger man who simply asked to be called Michel and who always and only called Christmas "*La Laide*" (which meant, Christmas was well aware, "Ugly One")—tromped for more than an hour into the densest part of the woods and rooted out the traps they'd previously hidden at the bases of several trees.

While her father and his friends struggled to pry open a rusted iron trap, Christmas busied herself by digging the leaves away from the base of another tree where she was sure they'd set another trap.

"*La Laide*," Michel hissed into her ear. "Come with me."

Christmas shook her head. "Busy."

"I need your help. Your hands are smaller, and there is a bit of a rabbit stuck in that trap over there," he said, gesturing at a nearby tree. Christmas rolled her eyes, but clambered up and followed the man to where he pointed. When they arrived at the tree, however, Michel pushed her to the mossy ground and lay on top of her. He pressed his face into the crook of her neck, inhaling deeply.

"No," Christmas said, writhing to push herself away.

"Christmas," he said. "Jesus, Christmas." His hand crawled up her waist to the side of her breast and clamped there, rough and painful. His thumb wandered toward her nipple.

"My father—"

"Your father told me I could have you if I would take you. You've grown too old and still nobody else wants you, *La Laide*. Your father is desperate to be rid of such an embarrassment." His hand crawled over her skin.

"Stop," she hissed. She wriggled her arm free and brought her thumb against the man's throat, pressing as hard as she could. He gurgled and his eyes went wide. He dropped his hands and knelt back, only for a moment, but long enough for Christmas to pull herself free and slither to her knees. In the next moment, he curled his hand into a fist and punched her in the mouth. Her front teeth slid out of place with a sickening crunch; she could feel pieces of them on her tongue, and the raw gum where they'd been rooted stung.

"*Stupide!*" he growled. He ran his palm across Christmas's chin, which prickled the stubble of rough, brown hair there. There was blood on her jaw, and he smeared it across her cheek with a sneer.

"Look at you, *La Laide*, you hairy ape. Nobody will want you."

Christmas did not mention that just moments before, *he* had seemed to want her very much, and probably would have taken her had she given herself to him. She hopped to her feet and kicked him hard in the belly before she turned and ran—without a word to anyone—all the way home. Her father, Christmas knew, would return furious from the expedition, tell her mother what she'd done, and the two of them would spend a long hour shouting bile at her and perhaps worse, so she crawled into the strongest, lowest branches of the pine tree behind the house and wept herself to sleep.

All night, she stayed hidden in the tree, and nobody came to find her. In the morning, when the sun had risen, she slipped from the branches and into the barn to begin her chores. Her father was sitting on a milking stool just outside the cow's stall, waiting for her. He stood. There was a freshly cut switch in his hand.

"Come here, Christmas," he said quietly.

"No," she said.

Henri took a step forward; the switch quivered with his movement.

"Come, now," he told her, patting his thigh as if calling a dog. Christmas shook her head and backed up toward the door of the barn.

"*Non, monsieur,*" she mumbled.

"You do not say no!" her father said. His voice was controlled and even, but rumbled underneath with rage. He hit the wall of the barn with the switch; it made a whipping sound on the air.

"*Non, monsieur, Papa,*" Christmas said. Her knees began to shake, and her right foot crept backward, ready to pivot and run, but she kept her eyes steady on Henri.

"You are *my* daughter! You will never say no!" her father shouted again. He seemed to have run out of ideas. He drew the switch back behind his head, ready to whip in her direction, but Christmas leapt backwards, turned on her toe and ran as fast as she could.

When her feet met the graveled dirt of the road, she kept running. When she found the edge of the woods, she kept running.

When she could no longer smell the pine trees, when the air stung her lungs and her stomach twisted in hunger, when the sky grew black and she could only see by the ambient light of the stars, she kept running, and did not stop until she was miles from home. She snuck into a rickety barn and crawled into the cow's stall, curled up in the hay, and warmed her hands under the cow's belly.

She slept there until morning, then began to run again. She ran for three days.

* * *

WHEN BARBUE WOKE IN HER trailer on the desolate morning, already knowing she would be without Minnie or Ramus or most of the

Attraction, she could hear nothing in the camp at all—no sound came from the trailer in which Olympia and Diamond slept, and there was no one else left to make noise. She heard no clanging of breakfast pots, no distant shouts of the riggers, no whinnying of impatient horses. The camp was empty and silent. Barbue pulled her hair into a knot at the back of her head, tied a gray shawl over her shoulders, and walked to the stream with a pail to gather the fish from the nets she had stretched across a shallow span of the stream the day before. She tied her skirt up around her hips, left her shoes on the shore, and waded into the water.

The net was full; perhaps six fish flapped desperately in its tangle, and Barbue happily pulled them each out by hand and dropped them, dry and struggling, into her pail. There would be food for the three of them for at least a couple days, just from a single afternoon's work. The stream bank was dappled with light, and what looked like fireflies or sun-glowing dandelion spores—tiny specks of light—flickered in and out of the shadows and lit the path ahead of her with a shimmer. Barbue smiled to herself because everything was yellow-green and fragrant and beautiful.

When she looked up, she saw, waiting for her on the path ahead, Michel, exactly as he was when she had known him: awkwardly tall, all limbs, with a rock-sharp Adam's apple, a brown fringed vest on his back, and a wiry black moustache on his lip. He stood smack in the middle of the path, so she could not pass.

"*La Laide*," he said, holding out a hand. "Come, now."

Her heart dropped. "No," she said, stumbling back.

"You will never say no, Christmas." Her father stepped from behind a tree to stand next to Michel.

"I am Madame Barbue." She took another stumbling step away from the men.

"*Madame?*" Michel scoffed. "You are *Mademoiselle La Laide*."

Her father stretched out his hands to her. "You are Christmas," he told her.

"No," Barbue told them. "I'm not any of that. No."

"You will never say no."

"No," she said quietly and stepped back again. She could feel behind her back the rough bark of a tree. She could not step back another time.

"Come here, La Laide," Michel said, shaking his head sadly, as if she had gravely disappointed him. "You have misbehaved." His hand curled into a fist at his hip.

"Go with Michel, Christmas," her father said.

"No." She said this louder, with more force.

"You will not say no to me, La Laide. I will not allow it. Perhaps your mother and father have been soft with you, but I will not be so. You may not say no," Michel said, and her father nodded and grabbed her arm. Michel took her other arm and they both pulled, until she was strung between them. They began to pull her toward the wooded path away from the stream.

Barbue struggled, kicking dirt as she twisted her body, but the grip of the two men was tight, and they held her fast. Shrieking through her head was a stream of *nonononono,* but she knew better than to let herself say it out loud. The time for talking to these men, for reasoning with them, was past; she could say nothing that would not make things worse, so she kept silent as she fought their hold. She kicked Michel on the tender back of his knee and he let go of her arm to grab his leg. Once her arm was free, Barbue twisted and jabbed her father in the eye so that he, too, let go, howling in pain. She pulled away from the men and lurched toward the stream bank.

"Come here, Christmas! Right now!" Though her father shouted and he was struggling in pain, his voice remained maddeningly calm, as if there could be no other choice but to comply.

"No," Barbue said under her breath as she waded into the shallows of the stream.

"Christmas! You will not say no! You will come here when I tell you to," her father growled, anger bubbling under his calm.

"*La Laide!* Do as your father tells you!"

Barbue stopped wading when she was waist-high in the stream and turned to face the men. She narrowed her eyes and stood still, though the water pulled and pushed, trying to take her with it downstream and away. She untied the shawl and let it be carried away by the water; she slipped her dress over her head and watched it float away like an awful gray spill. She pulled off her corset and every last bit of underclothing. Without the clothes, there was less pull on her body, and she felt freer and stood stronger. She saw her father hide his eyes from the sight of her bare body, but she no longer cared. She stood naked in the middle of the stream, refusing to cringe at the thought of being so exposed in front of the men, and she put her hands on her hips. Small fish and stream plants slipped against her bare calves. Cool air ruffled the hair on her arms.

From the shore came the faint calls of her father and Michel: "Christmas!" "*La Laide!*" The sound was like a cry of birds, barely audible above the rushing water. "My name is Barbue," she whispered. "I call myself Madame Barbue."

She heard the splashes of her father and Michel plowing into the stream and she moved, wading farther until she was up to her neck. The water tugged at her to continue, but she stopped and turned to look, for one last time, at her father. Clinging to his skin, his shirt was so soaked as to be transparent and spider-webbed black where the hair on his chest showed through. He pressed stolidly forward in the center of the stream, moving toward her, drawn sideways by the current but determined and fighting on. Michel pushed on right behind him; his face gathered in anger as he went.

"Come here, now!" her father shouted. "Be a good girl! Come along!"

Barbue realized she was not a good girl. She had never been a very good girl: she was stubborn most of the time—her father used to call her bullheaded, or sometimes *La Petite Mule*—and both her parents had made her well aware that she was neither beautiful nor sweet-tempered nor skilled in any useful work, useless at sewing, needlepoint, keeping house and stoking delightful conversation. Right now she was feeling violent and uncharitable as well. She turned her back on the men and pushed farther toward the rushing center of the stream. The water drew higher, splashing past her cheeks, nearly into her eyes.

"*La Laide!*" Michel called, his voice now desperately sweet, pleasantly distant. "*Ma cherie! Aimeé!*"

"No," Barbue said, tipping her chin back to be heard above the stream's rush. She went forward until the stream covered her head. She lifted her feet, relaxed, and let the water carry her weight down and away.

Fourteen
The Last Two People in the World

DIAMOND COULD NO LONGER HOLD enough rocks in her pockets to keep herself even close to the ground, so Olympia sewed a tube of fabric from Barbue's abandoned pillowcase and filled it with sand, and they wrapped it around Diamond's waist like a heavy belt.

"Stay," she said to Diamond early each morning, and Diamond, still sleepy, rolled over and mumbled. Olympia sighed and left the trailer with a pail on her arm to fetch them clean water for the day. It happened this way every morning for a week.

If she could avoid Diamond going outside at all, she preferred it, but Diamond was stubborn and insisted on fresh air and sunlight. On one such late spring afternoon, the two women took a walk into the woods so that Olympia could gather mushrooms and Diamond could breathe fresh air. Diamond still could not walk, since her feet didn't quite touch the ground, but the heavy belt Olympia had made kept her, at least, from floating off into the tree canopy. Olympia pulled her by the hand, stopping every once in a while to dig in the leaves at the base of a tree.

"We're going to run out of Minnie's money," Diamond said.

"We'll cross that bridge when we come to it," Olympia told her. "I can probably take in some sewing and maybe find work in someone's kitchen. I've done it before; it's not hard."

"I can't do much of anything when I'm like this." Diamond gestured at her own feet, which dangled two inches above the forest floor.

"You could probably do some sewing," Olympia offered. "We could weight you down in the trailer."

Diamond shook her head. "I never learned how to sew."

"I'll teach you," Olympia smiled. "I learned from Minnie, who was the absolute best."

She stooped to pull apart the ground cover of wet leaves and then to dig up the mushrooms she found underneath. Diamond pointed to the shore of the stream.

"Watercress!"

Olympia went to investigate, pulled a small bunch out of the shallow water, and sniffed it.

"It is," she said, then looked at Diamond. "We're going to be fine. We can find food. You know how to hunt, and I can fish. Everything will be fine."

"Everything will be fine," Diamond repeated as if convincing herself.

Olympia stood, kissed Diamond's nose, and touched her cheek fondly. "It will be fine. Even if the whole world disappears, and we're the only ones left in it," she said, then added, "That would be better than fine, actually."

"The whole world isn't disappearing, just all of us Attraction folks."

"Not all of us. You and I are still here."

"I don't know why. You're always fading, and I'm floating away," Diamond reasoned. "It doesn't seem like we have time to get comfortable. We're on our way out."

Olympia considered carefully. "We're not," she finally said. "Things are just changing. There's no circus anymore is all. We can't be a traveling show anymore. Or really any kind of show at all."

"We can't stay in one place. People will look too hard at us—two women alone, one who keeps disappearing and the other who keeps floating away."

"The disappearing comes and goes, and we're figuring out how to manage the floating. The tough part won't last. Things will change again. They always do."

"They could get worse," Diamond said.

"They could get better," Olympia said.

"Things haven't gotten better yet."

"Sure they have. Tomcat won't bother you anymore, and those awful clowns are gone, and I can kiss you and not worry about what anyone else suspects." With that, Olympia kissed Diamond on the mouth and wrapped her arms around her waist just above the sandbag belt. Diamond sighed, draped her arms over Olympia's shoulders, kissed her back, and decided not to mention her missing daughter, or all the others they loved who were gone now. It was a long, quiet kiss, and it felt to Olympia as if they both floated a bit.

"This is easy *and* hard," Diamond sighed. "Things are better *and* worse."

Olympia nodded and bent to root among the damp leaves for more mushrooms to put in her sack. "We could sell the mushrooms and the watercress."

"Who would buy that? It's food for country folk, and country folk find their own food."

"We could farm," Olympia offered. "Or at least make a little garden."

Diamond shrugged. It was a terrible idea for so many reasons, not the least of which was that Olympia would have to do all the work unless they could figure out a way to keep Diamond on the ground.

"Doing that would mean staying here."

Now Olympia shrugged. "We could try that," she said.

Diamond shook her head. "You couldn't do it. And the longer we're here, the more dangerous it will be, the more likely people will start to look in our direction, and the harder it will be to survive."

"We always found a way to get by before, even when nobody came to the Attraction."

"Before, there were more people pitching in. Before, we weren't all alone. Now, everyone is gone."

Olympia nodded. There was nothing she could say to that; it was true. She missed Barbue and Minnie, Arnold and Ramus the most, since the four of them had acted as her fierce guardians once her own parents had gone. Olympia shook the sack in which she'd been collecting mushrooms and watercress—it was nearly too full.

"We have more than enough here," she told Diamond. "Let's go back."

Diamond took hold of the back of Olympia's vest and allowed herself to be pulled along the wooded path. She rarely made the motion of walking anymore, but simply floated like a ghost, tethered to Olympia as she went. They walked like this until they could see the edge of the wood; the meadow beyond was yellow-bright with midday sun.

Olympia felt serene and wonderfully safe, so it was a rude surprise when Diamond tapped her shoulder and told her, "You're filtering out again." Before, she'd only start to disappear when she was extremely angry or frightened, or uncontrollably happy—when she was extremely *something*, anyway, and now she felt even-keeled and calm. But when she looked down, Olympia could see clean through her own skin; the dirt path was visible through her hands, making her look as if she were made of earth.

*   *   *

WHEN HER DAUGHTER WAS BORN, it was the most pain Diamond—Louise—had ever felt, as if she were being ripped open slowly over the course of an entire day. After several hours of fruitless labor, while her mother pressed cooling wet rags to her forehead and cooed encouragement in her ear, Louise was exhausted, and it seemed as if the hurting would never end, as if she would feel, for the rest of her life, this particular blend of tearing-apart metal-sharp pain and dull, grinding ache in every joint of her body.

"It's good," her mother said, rubbing her belly to ease the misery. "You need the pain. It will make you love her."

Every sensation felt too overwhelmingly sharp and clear; sounds were louder, almost painful to her ear, and even the brush of the wet rag against her face was an icy rasp. She cried against her mother's shoulder, mostly because she felt helpless to do anything else and because she could not imagine a time when the pain would be gone. Her husband waited anxiously in the parlor for news, though he never dared climb the stairs to the second floor of the house to visit the bedroom in which she labored.

Finally, the doctor decided to bring the baby out with forceps, because it had been hours and Louise had begun to cry pitifully and had lost all strength to continue the labor herself. When it was done, when the baby had been washed and swaddled and placed on her breast, when the pain had receded to a persistent, dull, twisting knot, Louise named the child Dahlia because her little face was as bright and round and open as the flowers in her garden. And then the two fell into exhausted sleep.

Her mother stayed with her for nearly a month, teaching Louise to feed and wash Dahlia and lull her to sleep. Still, the baby was most often red-faced and screaming when awake. Louise's mother was patient and calm; Louise wept, but kept trying, her teeth gritted and her vision swimming because she'd not slept well in days.

"Shouldn't a good mother know how to do these things?" Tom had asked when he'd had more than enough of his mother-in-law's presence and the child's crying.

"That's why my mother is here," Louise explained, trying to seem nonplussed while Dahlia wailed in her arms. "To teach me."

"A good mother would already know," he told her.

"Should a good father know it, too? Take her and calm her, if you think it can be done that easily." She held the crying baby out toward Tom, who said, "You've made this house impossible to live in," and stomped out of the room.

"It's not true," she whispered to Dahlia. "It's not true at all. We're both learning. I love you. Nothing here is impossible."

But the more time Louise spent with Dahlia, the less she slept, and the more desperate she felt. She began to hate the baby, which made her feel guilty and ashamed and, eventually, made her hate herself. It seemed as though Dahlia cried during most of her waking hours and her face was purple and angry in those moments when she wasn't crying, even while she slept. Every hour she woke again, screaming to be fed, and Louise was exhausted, sore, and wrung out. Her mother told her to hold the baby more closely to stop her crying, but Dahlia only wept louder when Louise clutched her tighter. Her face was constantly slick with saliva and snot, and it repulsed Louise to hold the writhing, angry little thing so close against her. When she did, the baby fought and pushed away and cried harder. Eventually, after more than an hour of screaming, Dahlia would tire herself out and fall asleep, a leaden weight against Louise's chest that kept her rooted to her spot and mindfully still, even to the point of pain, afraid to move and wake the baby.

*   *   *

IT WAS ALMOST AN ENTIRE year before Louise began to love Dahlia.

*   *   *

EACH MORNING, OLYMPIA AND DIAMOND made their way to the stream's edge to fish and gather greens and take a little air and sunlight. Diamond, heavy belt around her middle, still floated too much to walk, so she hung on to Olympia's arm and trailed behind her, just above the ground. Afterward, they spent the daylight hours working: tilling a small garden they'd started, cleaning their trailer, washing their clothes, cooking their food, sewing the piecework they'd taken in for a bit of money. In the evenings, when it began to get dark, they washed themselves in a basin of water and went to bed, where they lay undressed and drying together in a knot of skin and bone and muscle. Sometimes Olympia spent the night brushing her hand through Diamond's hair and trying to find the glitter of her eyes in the dark; sometimes they kissed for hours or made love softly until they fell asleep. All the while, Olympia held Diamond down and made sure to keep some part of her body on top of her to prevent her from slipping away into the air. Every day, Diamond was growing lighter and lighter, and it became harder to keep her close.

They rarely spoke anymore; they were so close, their bodies tied in such important balance that when Olympia disappeared, which happened from time to time, Diamond could always find her by feel, by the sound of her breath, and murmured soothingly until she began to filter back into view; Olympia kept hold of Diamond, rooted her so she would not slip out of bed and bang into the ceiling, or, when they fished, go floating off into the sky. They communicated by glance, by touch, by the shake of a head. There was, almost always, silence between them, which was delicately balanced as a clock, but this meant, too, that nearly everything they were thinking went unsaid. It was, for Olympia, both intimate and lonely.

At the start of their second week alone together, they walked to the stream to catch fish as they usually did: clutching hands, Olympia pulling Diamond along through the air near her hip. The sun had not yet risen, and the sky was a pale gray warming to pink at the horizon. When they entered the cover of trees, they had to make their way by the sound of the stream's watery babbling because almost no light penetrated the leaves.

Olympia gestured toward the stream with a nod, and Diamond pulled open the sack they'd brought for collecting watercress. She hooked her knees over Olympia's shoulders while Olympia squatted in the mud and began to gather the greens and drop bunches into Diamond's waiting bag. They worked like this for several long minutes, until Olympia looked up over her shoulder and smiled at Diamond. Diamond was peering into the bag, counting the bunches of cress they'd gathered so far. Her hair fell in stringy clumps around her cheeks. She was biting her lip. Olympia took her hand, shook the bag away, and pulled until Diamond leaned down. She kissed her, let her hands move up Diamond's hips to her waist, and kissed her again. Diamond, with a small noise, kissed back and nipped at Olympia's mouth until it was deliciously sore.

"This is good," Olympia sighed. "I love you."

Diamond smiled. "I love you, too," she said, and put her hands fondly on Olympia's cheeks. Olympia kicked aside the half-full bag of greens and pulled Diamond by the waist closer to the stream, wading in until she was almost up to her knees and Diamond's feet brushed into the water up to her ankles. Olympia began to bounce, dipping Diamond into the water halfway up her shins and threatening to go lower and dowse her completely.

"No!' Diamond laughed and kicked Olympia's legs. She slapped lightly at Olympia's shoulders. "Freezing! Don't you dare!"

Olympia laughed and bounced while Diamond squirmed.

"It must be done. We're both awful hot and awful dirty. Your dress is a shame," Olympia said.

"Don't you dare!" Diamond shrieked again and twisted so suddenly that the sandbag tied around her waist came loose, slipped off, and sank to the bottom of the river. Without thinking, Olympia let go of Diamond's waist to stoop and grab the sandbag, and without her hold, Diamond floated rapidly up.

"Olympia!" she cried. "No!"

Olympia, too late, realized her mistake, and stretched up to catch hold of something—anything—Diamond's toe or the hem of her dress—but she was moving upward too quickly and disappearing fast into the pinkening sky.

"Diamond! Try to kick for the trees!"

Diamond tried, flailing valiantly in the air, grabbing for tree branches that were just out of reach, but the more she struggled, the faster she floated. She kept slipping upward and was soon clear of the trees entirely, struggling in the air, getting smaller as she rose.

Before long, Olympia could no longer see her and could only hear the faintest crying of her name.

* * *

OLYMPIA LOOKED FOR DIAMOND FOR a long time, but found nothing. The sky was empty; the treetops showed no sign of her. She was entirely gone.

Olympia walked the dirt path back to her trailer, leaving the bag of cress and their fishing gear abandoned near the stream. She shut herself inside the trailer and sat down to wait for Diamond to return. She could think of nothing else to do. She thought about how she had watched Diamond disappear into the sky like a lost bird, flinging her limbs in a desperate and futile attempt to stop her ceaseless rise. It had been hopeless, but Olympia had watched, calling out, until she could no longer see Diamond; and even after that she'd squinted at the sky until the faint sound of Diamond's voice was gone, too, and there was nothing except the calm, gray expanse of air above the trees.

So Olympia sat and waited. She neither ate nor bathed nor attempted to put herself to bed. She hunched on the steps of the trailer as the night grew so black that the only light was dimly reflected from the stars, and still Diamond had not returned. The crickets made a ceaseless racket. The wind blew in the scent of moss from the stream's edge. Olympia's body began to ache from being so tightly hunched for so long, but still she waited, staring at the sky.

When the sun rose, and spilled everywhere in purple and orange, Olympia still sat on the steps. When noon burned hot and endless on her shoulders, still she waited. When the air turned blue again at sunset, she still had not moved from her perch.

She waited in that place for five days, through sunrises and sunsets, hunger and despair and exhaustion. She neither ate nor went to bed nor even allowed her thoughts to wander from their focus on Diamond and her unlikely return.

When she had given up and was finally gathering herself to stand, she saw a figure walking toward her from the line of trees. Though the sun had barely begun to rise and the air was still a dusky blue, Olympia was sure she could make out Diamond's wide frame and lumbering gait, and she leapt to her feet and went running, heedless of the pain.

"Diamond! You've come home!" she yelled, as the woman in the distance threw her arms wide and came running. They met in a crashing embrace, and Olympia would not let go of the woman even to let her breathe.

"Are you okay?" she asked, cupping Diamond's face and placing tiny kisses all along her jaw and neck. Diamond was crying, a hard, hiccupping and messy cry, and Olympia suddenly realized she was crying, too. "I waited for you, all this time."

"Thank you," Diamond whispered through her sobs. "I'm okay."

"Look at you." Olympia brushed the matted hair from Diamond's cheek. There were bright red scratches along her arms and across her face; she was dirty, her dress was torn, and she had no shoes. Olympia ran her hands down Diamond's arms, shaking her head at every new cut she found. After a moment, however, she froze, and squeezed Diamond's arms hard. "You're down! You're not floating up!"

"I stopped," Diamond said. "I floated for at least a day, until I thought I would die up there, and then I started to come down, a little at a time, until I was on the ground again. I don't know why."

Olympia shook her head, fresh tears clouding her eyes. "It doesn't matter."

"I didn't know where I was when I landed, except that I came down in the middle of brambles and trees. I walked until I found the stream, and then I followed that. I landed several towns over. I've been walking ever since."

"Without your shoes," Olympia said.

"I had no choice," Diamond told her.

Olympia held Diamond's hand for the rest of the night. She carried her to the stream and bathed her there, carefully washing the dirt from her face, gently patting the blood from the scratches. She fed her a simple dinner of fish and spoon bread, then carried her to the trailer and brought her inside. She peeled off Diamond's ruined dress and put her to bed, then curled up against her and lay her head near her shoulder. She was afraid to touch Diamond—every inch of her seemed bruised or scratched or sore—but she needed to be near her just the same.

"It's so good to be lying down in a bed," Diamond sighed. "When I was floating, I just hung there like a rag doll and couldn't sleep at all. And then I was walking and I didn't want to stop until I got to you. I never slept a full night; just napped along the way when I couldn't go anymore."

Pain rose in Olympia's throat as the muscles squeezed. Diamond suddenly drew a breath and sat straight up in bed, throwing Olympia off her side. "If I stopped floating, if I came back to normal, maybe it will happen for the others, too!" she exclaimed. "Maybe they'll all start to come back, Ramus and Barbue and Minnie! And Arnold, maybe Arnold will come home! And even the clowns! Maybe everything can be undone!"

"You're here now," Olympia said. The possibility seemed dim at best, and she wasn't entirely sure it was something she wanted anyway—it would be good to have Barbue and Minnie and Ramus back, but if that meant the return of the clowns, she wasn't convinced it would be for the best. She gently guided Diamond back down into the bed. "Rest."

"Maybe it can all be undone," Diamond mumbled sleepily, beginning to weep. "Maybe it can go back to before."

Olympia pressed her lips against Diamond's cheek and wept with her. They fell asleep like that, exhausted, sticky with tears, afraid to touch but afraid to move too far apart. Olympia kept her hand around

Diamond's waist; even in sleep, she was afraid to let go, too frightened of losing her again.

In the morning they slept late, finally rising when hunger got the best of them and returning to bed not long after they'd eaten. They spent two beautifully lazy days this way, until Diamond could rest no more. On the third day, they walked to town and bought new shoes for Diamond, as well as fabric to sew a new dress and a basket of apples, several of which Diamond managed to eat before they got back to the trailer.

The trip to town had, however, been too long a time spent in the company of others, too much effort to behave as others demanded, and all they wanted was to curl into each other and be alone. When they returned to the trailer, they put everything aside: The fabric was stored for sewing another day, and fishing and foraging for food was put off as well. They cast aside their clothes, dropped together onto the cot and did not leave the trailer again, but dozed in and out of kissing and whispering and holding one another. They neither ate nor bathed and looked at nothing but each other.

"You must never leave again," Olympia whispered.

"You must never disappear," Diamond countered.

"The world may end," Olympia said. "I won't ever leave you."

* * *

OUTSIDE, THE SUN ROSE AND set and rose again many times, the trees began to shake loose their leaves, the air grew cold and damp with the changing season, and still Diamond and Olympia could not leave their tiny home. They lay in the cot, their legs intertwined, their arms growing thinner, but neither woman could look away from the other's face, even for a moment. They lay clutching each other and did not think of eating or bathing or ever moving ever again.

* * *

Just moments before her parents disappeared forever, Olympia had been flying. The space at the top of the tent was dark except for the crazy swings of the spotlight and the occasional glint of sequins. Her father's teeth glowed when he smiled; her mother's eyes shone like new buttons. Her father flung Olympia into a midair flip, and her mother caught her and whispered in her ear, "*M'accroche, je m'accroche à toi, chèrie, toujours.*" The trapeze swung them in a long arc, and her mother deposited her safely back on the platform. Below, the audience applauded.

Her parents swung together and apart, flipped up to sit on their swings and pump their legs to propel themselves higher, then flipped back down to hang by their knees. It was work, she knew by their grunts, but they made it look effortless, like tossed and glinting coins, like silver flying fish, like slippery light. They called softly through the dark to each other; the sound was a river, that consistent and steady. She knew that if she jumped they would catch her. The net was there below, waiting, but they'd never once needed to use it.

Everything was motion: The spotlight slipped across the black air, her parents hurled themselves back and forth on the swings, even the audience below rumbled and churned in waves of excitement. She felt safest this way: everything flying, everything imminent. It was when the swings stopped, when they lost momentum and their arcs petered to nothing, that hanging on became hard and dangerous and far less beautiful.

She rarely needed, anymore, to concentrate on staying visible when she was on the swings. It was, like everything else in the air, intuitive and nearly effortless. On the ground was a different story—she still frequently faded or disappeared entirely, and had to be on her guard when walking through town with her parents to ensure that she didn't cause alarm by disappearing. But when she was on the swings, it was easy. She was lighter than air, and everyone else was so far away—the audience watched her, she knew, but only perceived a brief and fast-moving glint of sequins, light and movement and no detail. They might catch the flash of her smile, or the white of her arms arcing in the dark, but she was never still enough to really look at; she was so fast nobody could ever see all of her at once. Below, she could see a ripple of upturned faces craning for a better view like little round moons glowing in the dark.

Olympia stood on the platform and stretched her arms out, waiting to be caught and carried away.

Acknowledgments

IN ADDITION TO MY ENDLESSLY patient, loving and brilliant wife, to whom I've dedicated this book and without whom there'd be no book at all, I owe debt of gratitude to folks who had a hand in helping me: Annie and Candy and the stellar press they've built; C. B. Messer, who should design everything I write, including grocery lists; copyeditors Nicki and Zoe, who should also take a look at those grocery lists; language consultants Mo and Mer, who can help me translate those grocery lists into patois and French (neither of whom thought their contributions big enough to merit thanks, but both of whom are owed thanks anyway for helping more than they know); and any friend of mine unlucky enough to catch me in the mood to test out my ideas, to whom I probably owe several beers or cakes or bouquets. Which should probably be on those grocery lists.

About the Author

ALYSIA CONSTANTINE LIVES IN LOWER Hudson Valley, NY with her wife, their two dogs and a cat. When she is not writing, she is a professor at an art college. Before that, she was a baker and cook for a caterer and before that, she was a poet. Her debut novel *Sweet* is the 2016 Foreword Indies Award Honorable Mention for LGBT Literature.

For a reader's guide to **Olympia Knife** and book club prompts, please visit interludepress.com.

🌐 interludepress.com
🐦 @InterludePress
🇫 interludepress
🛒 store.interludepress.com

interlude  press™
you may also like...

Sweet by Alysia Constantine

Publishers Weekly Star Recipient

Alone and lonely since the death of his partner, a West Village pastry chef gradually reclaims his life through an unconventional courtship with an unfulfilled accountant that involves magical food, online flirtation, and a dog named Andy. Sweet is also the story of how we tell love stories. The narrator is on to you, Reader, and wants to give you a love story that doesn't always fit the bill.

ISBN (print) 978-1-941530-61-0 | (eBook) 978-1-941530-62-7

Sideshow by Amy Stilgenbauer

Abby Amaro has ambitions, but she's a good girl, and in 1957 good girls get married. She flees an overly possessive suitor to join a traveling carnival. Thanks to a burlesque aerialist and the world's saddest clown, Abby bides her time until she can return home. She doesn't expect a sideshow strongwoman named Suprema to capture her imagination.

ISBN (print) 978-1-945053-01-6 | (eBook) 978-1-945053-02-3

Luchador by Erin Finnegan

Publishers Weekly Star Recipient

A young exótico wrestler in Mexico City's professional lucha libra circuit charts a course to balance ambition, sexuality, and loyalty to find the future that may have be destined for him since childhood—a story about finding yourself from behind a mask.

ISBN (print) 978-1-941530-97-9 | (eBook) 978-1-941530-98-6

CPSIA information can be obtained
at www.ICGtesting.com
Printed in the USA
FSOW01n0040031117
40511FS

9 781945 053276